SON OF MANITOU

SON OF MANITOU

Albert R. Booky

REAL WEST

FICTION SERIES

Sunstone Press . Santa Fe . New Mexico

Dedicated to my son, Albert, and his wife, Terry

I wish to express my gratitude to my wife, Lee, for her neverfailing encouragement, advice, and support.

First Edition

Printed in the United States of America

Library of Congress Cataloging in Publication Data:

Booky, Albert R., 1925-
   Son of Manitou.

   I. Title.
PS3552.06436S6   1987   813'.54   86-23169
ISBN: 0-86534-097-8

Published in 1987 by SUNSTONE PRESS
           Post Office Box 2321
           Santa Fe, NM 87504-2321 / USA

FOREWORD

The mid 1800's was one of the most exciting and interesting periods in American history. This book contains the imaginary adventures of some enterprising and adventurous individuals who could have lived through those times.

The ranching families now living in New Mexico, in many instances, are descended from such stock, where the husband and wife worked as one to create homes for themselves and their descendents. They worked side by side, the women as self-reliant as the men. It was a hard life, but free of the bustling, turbulent, confining city life.

It was a time never to be matched in the history of the development of the American continent. It is the American epic, the American dream. It is difficult to realize that it, in fact, existed but it did, and in some areas it continues to exist.

Some of the characters in this book are historical individuals whose exploits are a matter of history.

Albert R. Booky
Lincoln, New Mexico
January, 1987

CHAPTER I

T he boy sat on a bench, his back pressed against the wall of the barn. His eyes shone with unshed tears as they sought the upper windows behind which the body of his beloved friend, General Andy Jackson lay. The friend he had known and revered had gone to join his beloved Rachel, and young Sam reminded himself of that and consoled himself with the thought. But without old Andy Jackson, the Hermitage would seem only a shell, whereas before it had been filled with the strength and spirit of the old general. Sam had been privileged indeed to have been closely associated with the general during his last years. He vowed to himself that whatever course his future life took, he would strive not to do anything which his old friend wouldn't have approved.

The sound of hoofbeats and the squeaking of a carriage being driven rapidly along the drive toward the entrance of the big house brought Sam out of his reverie. He saw a one horse buggy carrying three people sweep up the lane. A man drove and next to him sat a small child and a young woman. Their faces were drawn with worry and the fear that they might be too late. That they were fatigued was evident as they climbed from the buggy.

"That's Sam Houston!" The exclamation came from a groom as he trotted toward the house. "Now there's a man for you, young Sam Sidwell," he flung back over his shoulder.

Young Sam had heard that the famous Sam Houston was the closest thing that the old general had ever had to a son of his own. When the buggy swept to a halt in front of the house, a servant came out of the front door, shook Houston's hand, but shook his

7

head slowly from side to side, saying to the six-foot, six-inch giant, "You're too late, Mr. Houston, the general passed away about three hours ago."

The funeral over, young Sam packed his scanty belongings in his saddle bags and threw them behind his saddle. Then he led the trim, sleek young gelding toward the hitching rack near the house porch. He would pay his respects and then escape the forlorn atmosphere of the plantation. He tied his horse and entered the house, hat in hand and his head bowed slightly in deference to the old general's memory. He excused himself to the people in the parlor and told the friends and relatives of the late general that he was moving on, but that he would never forget his old friend's kindness. As he said goodby and walked out to mount his horse, a deep voice spoke behind him. He turned as Sam Houston continued, "Sam, the people in there," he motioned with his head toward the house, "said that you and the general were pretty close." He extended his hand to that of young Sam. "I too, was close to the general. We both had a rare privilege in knowing such a man."

Young Sam felt so inadequate as he stood in front of Sam Houston. He looked up into Houston's face as he said, "After the Indians killed my . . ." He had suddenly remembered that Houston was the adopted son of the Cherokees and so he stammered a bit, trying to finish what he had been about to say when Houston came to his rescue. "I understand, son," was his reassurance, "some things seem beyond reason."

"The general took me in," young Sam continued, "when I was only seven and raised me as if I had been part of his family. I'll never forget him and what he meant to me. His advice was the best. He never steered me wrong, and whatever I become will be because of him. I loved him so." His voice caught and tears came to his eyes.

Sam Houston's hand rested on the lad's shoulder as he said, "The general was one of a kind, incorruptible, honest to the point of perfection, and he was fearless. You probably know of the great influence which his mother had on him. He told me once that just before she died, she told him never to lie, nor to take what was not his own, and not ever to sue for slander, but to settle such matters himself. And he lived by those rules until he became president of these United States. When he became president, he felt he was no longer his own man, but belonged to the people. It wasn't easy for him with his hair-trigger temper, but he lived up to what he considered the bargain he had made with the people. Did you know he almost went into bankruptcy twice because he had to make good on notes which he had co-signed?

"Another time he had gone to the funeral of Representative Warren Davis from South Carolina, which was held in the Hall of Representatives. Suddenly, a man by the name of Richard Lawrence stepped out from behind one of the huge columns in the hall and fired a pistol at the president. Luckily the pistol misfired. At this, the president, cane in hand, went for the man. Lawrence pulled another pistol and aimed once more and again there was a misfire. The odds against having two pistols misfire like that are immense, but thank God for the president and for the country, it happened."

"Why did this fellow want to shoot the president?" asked young Sam.

"It was proven much later that the man was insane." answered Houston. "There was much anti-Jackson feeling at the time. The wealthy didn't like Jackson and the wealthy controlled the press, and it appears they controlled the pulpits also, to a great extent. You see, Sam, the general was a self-made man, never had any formal schooling, not one single day, and I think that the wealthy felt that only they, with their fancy schooling could govern, were fit to govern.

"Whereas the general trusted people like you and me, the more powerful did not. And then the power of the press is awesome. It called the general's administration, 'the reign of King Mob,' and influential senators such as Webster and Clay predicted chaos and disaster. In fact, Congressman Samuel Allen of Massachusetts said of him that it was '. . . putting forward a man of bad character . . . a man covered with crimes . . . than had ever been attempted before onto an intelligent people.'

"The Reverend Robert Little of Washington said, 'When Christ drew near the city, He wept over it!' Then when Harvard University bestowed an honorary degree upon Jackson, the degree of Doctor of Laws, John Quincy Adams said, 'Is there no way to prevent this outrage?' "

Sam Houston shook his head and continued, "These kinds of remarks may have given Lawrence the incentive to do what he attempted. We'll never know for sure, but it is possible. At any rate, Sam, the general proved to the world that one class of people can, without bloodshed or a revolution, gain political power. He was a great patriot and really loved this country and what it represents.

But did you know that when he left office he had exhausted all of his personal wealth for the good of the country? As a matter of fact, I wouldn't be surprised if he died still in debt. Let's hope that people like the general will come along now and then to keep this country on the right track!"

The two had begun to pace slowly down the long drive and young Sam said, "Tell me about his family, Mr. Houston."

"Well, his father died before he was born and he lost his two brothers, Hugh and Robert, in the revolution. The general fought in the revolution too. He was only thirteen, but that plucky rascal couldn't be kept out of any fight. He fought in the Battle of Hanging Rock. His mother died from typhus which she contracted while nursing some of the wounded soldiers."

Sam Houston mused as he stopped to fill his pipe. "'Old Hickory,' that's what they called him, or 'Andy by gosh Jackson.' When the general said he would hang someone if they disobeyed the law or his orders while he was in the military, they began to look for a rope! But I'm keeping you and you'll want to be on your way, young Sam," growled the towering Houston. "Where are you headed?"

"West," came the reply. "Tennessee has too many people for me. I want to see nature at its finest, where it hasn't been tarnished by man's ugly scars. I'd like to breathe air which no white man has ever breathed. You know what I mean, Mr. Houston! I'm not as worldly as you are and can't express myself as I'd like to, but I know what I want and in the West is where I believe I'll find it." The boy's face glowed with his vision and the older man's face was sympathetic. "Sam, I understand, and you're right. The West is for men of free spirit, such as yourself. My family and I are returning to Texas soon and we would like for you to return with us. Texas could use young men like you. I have many . . ."

Before Houston could finish, young Sam interrupted, saying, "Thanks, Mr. Houston, but I want to find my own way, my own life, at my own speed. I want to test my skills, my strength, and my endurance against the elements of mother nature and that of all enemies of mankind. I have a feeling for adventure that has been locked up in me and is fighting to get out. I must free that spirit and let it take its course. It may lead me to Texas some day, but I want, I must let it be free to go where it wishes. Mr. Houston, I mean no disrespect, especially to you, but do you understand what I'm trying to say?"

"Yes," Sam Houston said with a smile on his lips, and young

Sam could see in his eyes that spirit akin to the one which was locked up in himself.

"Thank you, sir," young Sam said, with the deepest respect. "I'd better be on my way. I hope I can make General Jackson proud of me." He mounted, spurred his horse lightly and waved at Sam Houston as his horse loped away from the Hermitage. Houston watched until the youth disappeared through the trees.

Sam rode at a walk as he followed the path through a forest thick with underbrush. He could see only a few feet before the trees, brush, vines, and other vegetation blended into a solid wall of green. He knew that he was somewhere near the Natchez Trace, the trail about which he had heard so much from the old general. It was a heavily traveled trail northward from New Orleans. Settlers along the Ohio and upper Mississippi Rivers made rafts of logs to transport their goods by water to New Orleans and after selling their merchandise and rafts, by using the Natchez Trace, they returned home either on foot or on horseback along the Mississippi and Ohio shorelines. The Trace was traveled by robbers of every description intent on preying on the homeward bound settlers.

The most horrible scream jarred Sam from his thoughts, chilling his blood as it vibrated through the forest. He reined in his horse, listening, thinking it would come again. When it did not, he dismounted and tied his horse to a tree with a stout rope and moved cautiously in the direction from which he had heard the scream. He crouched and carefully parted the undergrowth soundlessly as he moved farther into the forest. In a few minutes, he could hear voices and he slowly lowered himself to the ground and lay there motionless, waiting for the voices to give him their location. He didn't have to wait long, for to his left the sound of muffled voices came once more. Sam crawled in that direction moving so slowly and carefully that he scarcely made a sound. Then he heard a loud splash and a voice asked, "Is the other one ready?"

Sam moved a small limb on the bush in front of him very slowly as he heard another voice say, "Give me a hand here, Tim."

What Sam saw almost made him vomit. The two men apparently had come upon a camp of traders on their way back up the Trace with the proceeds received from their trading. The men, one holding a dead man's feet and other his shoulders, were carrying him toward the river. The dead man had been stripped to the waist and Sam could see that he had been gutted and then a large stone had been sewn into the cavity created, thus ensuring that the body would never rise to the surface. Within a few seconds the dead man had been thrown into the river and immediately disappeared under the water.

"No one will ever find them," laughed one of the men as he turned to walk back to the campsite. "Come on, Tim, let's see what we'll find this time," and he beckoned to his companion. They froze suddenly in their tracks and listened to the sound of hoofbeats nearby, then moved swiftly into the brush only a few feet in front of Sam.

"We left our rifles leaning against the tree over yonder," Tim muttered to his companion.

"What we'll do then is jump him as he comes by us on his way toward the camp," the other decided.

"Right," agreed Tim.

The horseman came closer and then halted, apparently sensing something wrong, but then the hoofbeats could be heard again as the horseman rode into the clearing. Sam's eyes widened as he saw that it was a young Indian brave. He sat his horse proudly, eyes searching the camp. His horse's ears pricked forward, toward the underbrush and the youth readied his rifle; then in a flash he had whirled to meet the danger as the two men leaped at him, an ill-considered move under the circumstances. The boy's first shot knocked Tim backward with such force that it picked him off his feet and he landed in a small clump of oak brush, face up, with his knife still clenched in his fist.

At this moment, Sam sprang forward to the tree where the men had left their rifles, seized one, aimed, and pulled the trigger before the man could drive his knife a second time into the Indian youth. The man hesitated a moment, then fell across the figure of the Indian. Sam dropped his rifle and ran to the wounded youth, rolling the body of the robber away. The eyes of the Indian met Sam's for a second before they closed. Sam saw that the knife wound was just below the left collar bone. He swiftly tore his own shirt and made a pad with which he staunched the flow of blood, then placed a small rock upon the pad to keep it in place while he searched the camp for something to cleanse the wound. He found a partly filled whiskey bottle leaning against a log near the fire. This should do it, he thought, and then searched further for something with which to bind the wound securely. At length, he found a white dress which one of the settlers must have purchased for his wife in New Orleans. This he tore in strips and then returned to the lad, removed the pad and slowly poured the whiskey into the wound. The young brave stirred and moaned, but otherwise didn't regain consciousness, as Sam bandaged the wound the best way he knew how.

CHAPTER II

T he young Indian brave opened his eyes and felt of the blanket which covered his body to his chin. He could smell food cooking and he slowly turned his head toward the fire. He saw a stalwart, tanned young man sitting on a log by the fire as he turned a turkey on a spit. The Indian lad tried to sit up, but he was too weak, and sank back to the pallet. A smile crossed Sam's face and he stood up and moved toward the Indian. "Well, you're a tough fellow, aren't you?" He knelt to inspect the wound. "My name's Sam, and you're lucky I came along when I did or you'd be long gone by now."

The Indian said nothing, just looked at Sam.

"Do you speak English?" Sam next asked as he returned to the fire to turn the meat once more.

"Yes, like a white man," the lad replied.

"Good. Do you think you could sit up with my help and have a little something to eat?"

"You're not any older than I am," the Indian observed as Sam helped him to lean against a nearby tree trunk.

"I suppose not," Sam grinned.

"How long have I been out?"

"Not long," Sam said with a warm, friendly smile, "you're weak from losing more blood than you could spare; all you need now is something to eat and you'll be fine."

As the two ate, they exchanged histories in shortened version, and Sam found that the youth was half Mandan and half white. His father had been a mountain man who had married an Indian woman and become a 'squaw man' as most white men termed it. The youth was called by many a half-breed or 'breed' for short. His father had come back to civilization to sell his furs and then to see his sister, whom he hadn't seen for many years. But before he could sell his furs and go on to Missouri to visit his sister and show off his son, he was killed by some townspeople. "He should have sold our furs at the rendezvous, as we'd always done before," the youth told Sam sadly, "the American Fur Company always paid us a good and fair price."

"You haven't told me your name yet," Sam remarked, "why not?"

"I have no name, and won't have until I have performed an heroic deed. That is the law of my people, the Mandan."

"You have just performed an heroic deed against those two outlaws," retorted Sam. "Why don't you call yourself Lone Wolf? May I call you that?"

"That would please me," came the reply.

"Good, that's settled. I'm Sam and you're Lone Wolf," Sam said with satisfaction. "Now those outlaws killed some people, at least two for sure, and threw their bodies into the river. I did the same to theirs after I searched them. There must be horses around somewhere. The outlaws must have had two, maybe more, and the murdered men had several, to judge by all of these supplies. I've found shovels, picks, blankets, pots and pans, twenty-six Sharpes rifles and enough ammunition for them to last at least a year. Also a dozen double-bitted axes and twenty-one pistols with ammunition, plus boots, beaver hats, and one large wooden box filled with an assortment of knives, at least fifty, and oh yes, I almost forgot, there were two boxes of tomahawks!"

"What do you think they were going to do with all these supplies?' asked Lone Wolf.

"It's my guess," replied Sam, "that these people were merchants and probably lived on a frontier where barter is used. The frontier folks usually barter for what they need, and that's why I reckon the poor devils that were killed had to be merchants. Whoever they were, we'll never know, for I've searched the camp and could find nothing to identify them. The outlaws must have left their identification on them or maybe burnt it."

"Well, I guess the next thing to do is try to locate those horses," suggested Lone Wolf.

"You stay here and watch the camp, and I'll scout around for the horses; you need to get your strength back for our journey west."

"West!" exclaimed Lone Wolf in astonishment. "Are you going west, too?"

"Where else would I be going?"

"Then you must come with me to see the village of my mother, at the big bend of the Missouri River where it turns west," Lone Wolf said excitedly. "You would bring honor to me and my people if you would do this."

"I've no special place to go, so I'll take you up on your offer, but if we don't find those horses, we'll never get started, so I'd better look for them."

That night before the fire, the two young men discussed their early lives while twelve horses including their own, watched from the long rope which was stretched between two trees. They had been found hobbled and grazing on a meadow knee deep in grass not far from the river. Two of the horses were Clydesdales, the young men figured from their huge size and build, and the rest were good sturdy ponies, so the two were well pleased.

"My people, the Mandans, will not believe their eyes when they see those two big ones," Lone Wolf said as he studied the big, gentle horses. "Those two alone, will make us legends for all time! Warriors will be talking about them and us around the camp fires from many moons." He sat near the fire cross-legged, one hand resting on a knee and the other holding his father's pipe a few inches from his mouth as he blew smoke upward. "You know," he said as he watched Sam lay some more wood on the fire, brush the bark from his sleeves and then attempt to lower himself cross-legged in imitation of Lone Wolf, "tobacco is a good thing . . . it smells good, it relaxes you. Here, try some Sam," the Indian said as he extended the pipe to Sam.

Sam hesitated a moment, then inserted the pipe between his teeth and inhaled at the same instant, coughed and removed the pipe, coughing again as he handed it back to Lone Wolf. "I guess it could be an acquired taste."

Lone Wolf laughed softly as he accepted the pipe and began to puff once more. "You'll learn to love the taste, my friend, and one day you'll be as my father and the Indians. The Indians say that 'cigar' relaxes you and makes you sleepy as well as being an enjoyable pastime. You know, Sam, cigar or the Spanish term, 'tobacco' is believed by the Indians to have been given to them by the mighty Manitou. The Indians believe that Manitou made earth and everything on it and that the last and worst creature he put on earth was man. That he gave man cigar to contact him. If man smoked cigar or tobacco, Manitou would listen."

"Do you suppose man is an abbreviated form of Manitou?"

"I never thought of it that way; you know Sam, it may very well be. I'll ask my mother when we get to my village."

"Let me try that pipe again," Sam said as he reached for the pipe. After a few small puffs, Sam could smoke without coughing and after that they passed the pipe between them.

Finally Sam leaned back on one arm and with a long stem of grass in his mouth remarked, "You'll have to teach me to speak Indian."

"That is impossible," came the Indian's reply.

"I'm not that slow," came Sam's indignant answer as he rose back to a sitting position.

Lone Wolf chuckled, "Tell me, Sam, can you speak 'white man'?"

"Sure, I'm speaking it right now."

"You're speaking English, not 'white man'," Lone Wolf grinned as he threw a small pebble at Sam.

"Oh," Sam said with comprephension, "Yeah, you're right; I see what you mean. German, French, Spanish, and Greek are all white men's languages, and English is just one of the them, and so it is with the Indians."

"I can teach you to speak the Mandan tongue, which is related to the Sioux. You see the Mandan is one of the Sioux tribes, part of the Sioux nation. Sam, if we are going to get an early start in the morning, we'd better get some sleep. I'll take the first watch."

Sam watched Lone Wolf walk to a tall tree and sit down, leaning against its trunk and laying his Sharpes across his lap. Lone Wolf wore moccasins laced with beadwork, long trousers which were a curious combination of the chaps of a cowboy and the animal skin pants of a mountain man. Animal fur of some kind was stitched along the outer seams and was red in color. Over his bare chest and shoulders, a colorful blanket was wrapped. His hat was pure 'mountain man' tall and furry, with a feather inserted at the back.

The following morning, the two young men packed the supplies which they had accumulated onto the horses and headed westward. The two lead horses were the Clydesdales who were followed by the others. Sam led the procession, while Lone Wolf rode ahead to scout. In a short time, Lone Wolf rode back to tell Sam that he had located a ferry crossing the mighty Mississippi

River.

The ferry was owned and operated by an old man together with his wife, three sons, and a daughter. The wife and daughter provided food and lodging if requested.

Three men were lounging outside of the lodge as Sam and Lone Wolf approached the landing. The three studied the young men and their pack animals, and their curiosity caught Lone Wolf's attention. "Be ready to defend yourself at a moment's notice."

Sam glanced at Lone Wolf to show his agreement with his assessment.

Lone Wolf dismounted and adjusting a pack, continued, "If we have trouble, it could happen soon, or they may wait until we've crossed the river and are away from the ferry, but we'd better be prepared."

"Howdy," said the old man as he drew near. "Going west?"

"Yes, how much will it cost us to get to yonder side of the river?" asked Sam as he nodded toward the far side.

Lone Wolf sat motionless as Sam stood in his stirrups, his eyes searching the opposite bank.

"Twenty-five cents for each horse, loaded or empty, makes no difference what's on their backs."

"Fair enough," Sam agreed, "we'll want to cross right away."

"As soon as I have your money, you'll be on your way, less you want some of my wife's stew," the old man suggested as he motioned toward the smaller of the cabins. "But on second thought, if I were you two, I'd want to cross first and eat later." He nodded toward the three men.

"Boys, let's get these horses across!" He accepted the money from Sam and turned to help his sons. The three boys seemed nervous and Lone Wolf sensed it, although Sam didn't seem to notice.

"Ready to load, pa," one of the boys called.

The horses were loaded onto two log rafts and began to cross the river slowly. When they had reached the western side, Sam and Lone Wolf unloaded and waved their hands to the old man on the other side. The three boys who had accompanied them began to use their poles as they attempted to keep the rafts from drifting down the river. The only comment one of them made was, "If this were spring runoff, you wouldn't be able to cross."

They waved as they slowly moved away from the river landing toward the opposite shore.

"Did you notice the looks in their eyes?" Sam went on, "Those boys are scared to death."

Lone Wolf didn't answer immediately, for he was studying the three men as they huddled together, apparently discussing something earnestly.

"What do you think?" Sam asked again.

"I think," replied Lone Wolf, "that we'd better make a return visit to help that old man and his family."

The two young men rode into the forest which grew close to the river bank as if they suspected nothing, but after that they rode up the river until they reached a good location to tie their horses. Then they made their way back to the river bank which was quite a way upstream now from where they'd crossed. They could see the cabins in the distance as they searched for anything to use to help them navigate the river. They came across a fallen tree finally which they deemed sufficient to use to cross the sluggish river. As the boy had said, if this were spring runoff their plan would not be feasible. They judged that they had ridden far enough up river to be able to land not far from the ferry landing. They crossed the river as planned, and Lone Wolf moved first toward the rear of the cabin, running in crouched position for about thirty yards, then falling to the ground. Sam could see his hand as it waved him forward. This procedure continued until they had reached the back of the cabin. Lone Wolf motioned to Sam to follow him as they heard voices from inside the cabin.

"For the last time, old man, where is the money? If you don't tell us now, your daughter will die first."

"Could I have a little fun first?" Another of the voices spoke in a whining drawl.

It was at this moment that Lone Wolf and Sam reached the front corner of the cabin and Lone Wolf peered around the corner, seeing that the door of the cabin was ajar. He motioned to Sam to be ready as he pulled his knife from its sheath. Sam moved to his side and at an agreed upon signal, they dashed into the cabin. As they rushed in, the old man and his family were seen to be lined up on the left hand side of the room and two of the three men were to the right, their backs toward the door, with their rifles ready. The third man was on the family's side of the room, making a lunge at the daughter. Sam and Lone Wolf plunged their knives into the backs of the two men and they sank to the floor. It wasn't as easy to reach the third man for the oldest son was between them. On a reflex, the third man howled at the intruders and fired, hitting the son, but before the boy had fallen completely to the floor, Lone Wolf had sunk his knife into the chest of the third man.

The wounded boy was sitting up in bed with his back resting against the crudely constructed headboard when Lone Wolf came back from disposing of the dead men and asked, "How is he?"

"Just a flesh wound in his right shoulder," Sam said with satisfaction.

"Good."

"How can we ever repay you?" The boy's father extended his hand to Lone Wolf as he rose from a chair near the bed.

"By taking us back across the river?" suggested Sam.

"Not on your life!" The old man laughed and continued, "at least not until ma has a chance to feed you. Now you've got time for some of her good stew."

As they were crossing the Mississippi River for the third time in a few hours, they found out more about the old man and his family and why they had elected to settle here. They were from Cincinnati, Ohio which was sometimes referred to as Porkopolis. The old man said that the squeals of the pigs could be heard all over the city, that pigs even roamed the streets as scavengers.

The old man told them that he had worked at the processing plant, but after a few years he had told himself that there had to be a better way to earn a living. As he described the slaughtering process, his listeners could understand readily his need to make his living in the outside world, in the sun and wind, and among green, growing things.

"You ought to have a better system to protect yourselves, though," Sam cautioned as he shook the old man's hand in farewell.

"You're right about that, young fellow, this whole episode has taught us that."

CHAPTER III

The two young men made an average of thirty-five miles a day for the next few days, keeping mainly along the banks of the Missouri River, thus using the shelter of the great trees and bushes for concealment from any enemies. At night the lush grass provided plentiful forage for their horses, which they hobbled, with the exception of one which they kept staked out on a long rope not far from their camp. A horse was always handy that way to use to bring in the others each morning at daybreak. Fish and game provided them with ample food and the berries which grew wild everywhere gave an added zest to their diet.

Evenings around the fire gave the two a chance to learn, in the case of Sam, and to teach, which became the function of Lone Wolf.

Sam learned that the Mandan Indians lived in two small villages along the bluffs of the upper Missouri. They were farming people, raising corn, squash, and beans. Their language was that of the Sioux nation. Lone Wolf's mother had told him they were the first Sioux tribe to be driven onto the plains by the westward push of the white man. Before the white man came, the Mandan had been a large tribe, maybe over a thousand people, but with the white man came disease, smallpox, which had nearly destroyed the Mandan as a people. Only about one hundred fifty people now remained.

"With so few," Sam asked, "how can they survive?"

"They are Sioux, and the Sioux are still many," explained Lone Wolf.

The two young men spent many hours talking beside their small campfires, small so as not to attract those who might be curious. And when they slept, they slept well away from their fire for safety's sake.

"Tell me more about your people," Sam said as he knocked his pipe lightly on a nearby rock. While he was refilling it, he noticed that Lone Wolf was watching him, chuckling. "You leave a good sign," grinned his friend.

"What do you mean?"

"Indians who come upon our camp will know it was a white man's camp."

"How could they tell?"

"Indians do not smoke while they are on the move; only white men leave tobacco ashes around the campfire."

"That's one thing I'll remember," Sam said, "I would appreciate it very much if you would teach these things to me as you think of them."

"It's the least I can do for you after you saved my life."

That night as Sam lay rolled in his blanket, he was awakened by a nudge. He opened his eyes and saw the moccasined foot of Lone Wolf and instinctively Sam jerked his blanket away and picked up his rifle. Lone Wolf had his index finger across his lips. He then raised his right arm at the elbow and moved it across his chest, where it became stationary. With the index finger of his left hand, he slowly moved it across the upper part of his clenched fist repeatedly. The sign for Indians.

Sam quietly rose to his feet, checked his rifle with a glance and then his eyes returned to his friend. Lone Wolf now extended the fingers of his right hand and placed his index fingers across the extended fingers. Sign language for horses . . . the Indians were after the horses. The horses were restless and Sam heard a nicker. Lone Wolf pointed to the trees up river, indicating that the Indians were in that direction. He pointed to his nose as he raised his head and sniffed in that direction. Sam did the same and on the third sniff, a small smile creased his face. He could smell them! The odor was a combination of things, but mostly of grease, maybe bear grease, and animal hide.

Lone Wolf raised three fingers, then quickly lowered them and quickly raised five fingers. Sam nodded, three to five Indians, Sam told himself. Lone Wolf pointed for Sam to circle around in back of the horses and then pumped his hand up and down in a rapid motion, quickly, Lone Wolf meant.

Sam crouched and disappeared into the underbrush and Lone Wolf also crouched in the brush and waited for a sign or sound. A twig snapped to his left and he slipped his knife from its sheath, seeing a small bush barely move. Lone Wolf couldn't see anyone, so surmised that the Indian was crawling on his stomach. He waited patiently, and then in a few seconds he could see a hand very slowly moving forward to his left. The hand very carefully explored the ground in front of it for its next move. The brush was so thick that its owner could still not be seen. The hand withdrew and Lone Wolf decided that the Indian was moving in another direction. Then he heard breathing and realized that the quarry was standing, ready to strike. He quickly raised his eyes, and through the leaves of the bush in which he was concealed, he could see part of a face, a face whose eyes were searching to its right and then to its left, over Lone Wolf's head. I am not the only fool, Lone Wolf told himself; he does not look down. I'll have to move fast, before he does. He moved rapidly, rising to his knees and at the same time throwing his knife through the leaves. The eyes of the enemy turned downward at the sudden noise but then disappeared and there came the sound of leaves rustling and a body falling. As Lone Wolf reached his enemy, he found him lying on his back, the knife to the hilt in his chest. He saw Lone Wolf and tried to rise, then sank back, dead. Lone Wolf pulled his knife from his opponent and fell to his knees once more a short distance away, listening, as his eyes searched for any sign of further movement. Pawnee, he told himself, as he glanced back at the dead man. He resumed his survey as he wondered how Sam was faring.

Sam had reached the rear of the restless horse herd and was searching for a sign of the thieves when a thud behind him caused him to whirl and duck. An Indian brave stood poised there, tomahawk in his right hand and he sprang as Sam whirled and dodged, but Sam wasn't fast enough and the Indian's body threw him to the ground, but the Indian had a knife between his shoulder blades.

Sam's first thought was Lone Wolf, but before that thought had a chance to register properly, he saw the shadowy figure of a man step forward from the bushes, saying, "That's the last one. The other cashed in a few minutes ago, and your friend got the third."

Sam rolled the body of the Indian away and rose, looking up at a mountain man. The long hair which fell from under his fur hat was red, as red as the sun. He wore Indian leggings to the knees, leather breeches, and a fringed buckskin shirt which was opened half way to his waist, the rawhide strings which usually laced up the shirt dangled from the bottom holes. His face was burnt from many seasons of sun and wind to a reddish brown, speckled with freckles, as close as one with his coloring would get to brown, and he wore a short, red beard. A tomahawk was lodged under his leather belt, and a rifle was cradled under an arm. As he leaned forward to pull his knife from the dead Indian, he wiped the blood off on the grass and remarked, "Tell your friend they have all crossed over."

"Crossed over? Crossed over what?"

"Gone under," the mountain man grunted.

"Lone Wolf," Sam yelled, "over here!"

The mountain man bent and neatly took the scalp of the dead Indian in a fashion that Sam realized was not his first. With one incision, his knife lifted the scalp, leaving the Indian with a bloody, bald head. The scalplock took the left ear of the Indian with it, as the mountain man's strong fingers ripped it off the head.

The three men sat eating the venison which the hunter had taken from one of his packs. The newcomer's name was Thor Elkinson, he told them, between bites. Sam and Lone Wolf introduced themselves in turn.

"You're a breed, ain't ya?" Thor stared at Lone Wolf as he wiped his whiskers with the back of his hand. His other hand held a large piece of deer meat. His eyes stared at Lone Wolf, never blinking, until Lone Wolf answered.

"Who was your father?"

"McClan, Jim McClan," Lone Wolf told him.

"Well, I'll be, so your Jim's papoose. Why aren't you traveling with your pa?"

"He's dead."

Thor stopped chewing, looked again at Lone Wolf and asked, "How, where, by who, and when?"

When Thor had been told all of the details, his only reply was, "Good man, damn good man; we'll all miss him. He could shoot as straight as an arrow, and he never missed. Civilization will kill any man. Beaver Pelt, your ma, she doesn't know about your pa, you know."

"How do you know this?" It was Lone Wolf's turn to be

24

surprised.

"She was worried about the both of you and when I came into the village, she . . . well I figured since I was headed this way, I'd check on your whereabouts, and besides I owed Jim that much. We trapped together one season up on the Yellowstone. That's before both your times, though. Them were good times. Not many white men in them parts in them days. Now they're crawling like ants all over the country, ruin everything before it's over."

Thor drew on his pipe and continued, "You've got a precious cargo, boys; it would make any Indian a chief if he were to lay hands on it. Until now you haven't been detected and if you can keep it that way, you will keep your hair as well as your cargo, but if it gets out, Indian braves will swarm over you like bees over honey. One more week and you'll be at the bend of the Missouri, with your ma and her people. In that case you two will be big medicine to the Mandans. But if we were to mosey along a little more rapidlike we might make it to the village in three or four days, provided we were careful."

"Provided we're careful? Are you going with us?" asked Sam.

"Them's my intentions, if there's no objection?"

"No objections!" Lone Wolf answered quickly.

Thor told them that if Lone Wolf and he rode flank a few miles from the river and Sam stayed under cover of the trees with the horses, better time could be made. No fires at night, and no travel at night. It would be too difficult to spot danger at night. Two would keep watch at a time during the night while one slept. If a buffalo herd came along, it could carry the horses with it, if the horses spooked and got mixed up in the herd. Thor told them that cattle down in Texas were lost this way from what he'd heard, so if a buffalo herd came too close, Sam should keep the horses in the river bottoms while he and Lone Wolf tried to spook the herd in the opposite direction. They would have no choice, though this had the obvious drawback of attracting any Indians nearby. Indians realized that stampeding buffalo or even trotting buffalo was a sure sign of something unusual. Either a prairie fire or maybe other Indians in their hunting grounds, killing buffalo, so they'd be sure to hit the trail to see what had caused the disturbance. Thor knocked out his pipe on the trunk of the tree he was leaning against and said, "If there are no questions, I suggest Lone Wolf ride south of the river and I'll ride north. We have many hours of daylight to take advantage of and those hours could make the difference."

CHAPTER IV

On the third day, smoke from the Mandan village could be seen by the three men. Thor reined in his horse sharply, and Lone Wolf sensed it at the same time. Sam looked inquiringly at each in turn. They sat motionless in their saddles, listening, and then suddenly Lone Wolf yelled at his horse and dashed off at a full gallop toward the village.

"What's going on?" Sam looked at Thor.

"When you live here in the mountains long enough, you can sense when things aren't right. I could sense it and so could Lone Wolf. I let him go because it's his village, and you couldn't be left alone with the horses. There's trouble and death in the air."

The two of them kept moving toward the village, but increased their speed to a steady trot. When the village came into sight, Thor and Sam could see warriors galloping toward them and Sam gave Thor a quick glance and checked his rifle.

"No need for that, Sam, they are Mandans."

Sam looked at Thor, then back at the charging Indians, then back at Thor. The Indians rode up and surrounded Thor, Sam, and the horses. They had come as a protective escort to the village. The lead Indian raised his right arm, bent at the elbow. His index finger and the one next to it were extended, and the other two were folded back toward the palm of his hand, held there by his thumb; the Indian sign for friend. Thor returned the same sign of friendship.

Chief Yellow Horn met them at the entrance to the village, riding his paint horse, and welcomed them.

The village had a wall around it which was constructed of

upright logs, forming a stout stockade. Inside the wall, Sam could see a number of dwellings which were roofed in dirt. They resembled Eskimo igloos, but they were larger. Some of them were constructed of hides, but all of them had the round, dirt roofing. Indians were busily engaged in many tasks. Some of them carried wounded men, while others seemed to be preparing for an attack by someone.

While Lone Wolf went in search of his mother, the others learned that the village had been under attack until the attackers had seen them approach and had withdrawn. Apparently they had imagined that a large party of Sioux were coming to the aid of the Mandan from the amount of dust kicked up by the pack animals.

"They have not gone far," Thor told Sam. "We're in for another attack as soon as they reorganize, most probably in the morning, at sunup."

Thor, Lone Wolf, and Sam uncrated the rifles, showing them to the surprised and happy Mandan warriors. In one bundle of rifles, Sam saw stamped on the box the words, "special order." He called Thor and Lone Wolf over as he brought out the finely engraved weapons.

"How many are there?" inquired Lone Wolf.

"Four," was Sam's reply.

"Give the fourth to Yellow Horn."

During most of that night, the Mandans were given lessons in how to load and fire the weapons. Extra shells were distributed to each rifle owner and the men were stationed at the wall as they awaited the dawn and another attack by the Blackfeet.

Thor and Sam sat near an open fire not far from the wall, while Lone Wolf leaned against a gate post and stared at the probable direction from which they could expect the Blackfeet. He suddenly turned toward Sam and Thor and spoke, "I've thought of a plan and I want your opinions, both of you."

"Let's have it," Thor leaned forward.

"What the Indian does not understand, he believes to be the work of the gods. Why not use this superstition to our advantage? The Blackfeet have not seen the Clydesdales, nor do they know we have the rifles. The last charge they made against my people was repulsed with arrows. Now, I'll hide one of the Clydesdales in that clump of bushes over there." His finger pointed to a thick growth not fifty yards from the stockade. "For at least one hundred yards, and in some cases even more, land is clear around the village. I will find a small, the smallest horse I can get of the same color as the

Clydesdale, among my people. You two will find a way to lead the Clydesdale to those bushes while it is still dark, tie him there, and return undetected.''

''How?'' Sam pondered

''I'm sure you're resourceful enough to do that,'' Lone Wolf grinned. ''In the morning, I will ride out toward the Blackfeet on the small horse to perhaps twenty or thirty yards of the bushes. There I will gain the attention of the Blackfeet.'' Lone Wolf laid the entire plan before Sam and Thor and they grinned, agreeing that it was well worth a try.

As the sun began to climb above the tree tops, the Blackfeet were surprised to see a lone Mandan sitting astride his horse perhaps fifty yards in front of the stockade. He carried a circular shield strapped to his left shoulder and in his right hand he held a decorated lance. He sat motionless, head lifted toward the sun.

The Blackfeet gathered under the cover of the trees and brush to watch and try to decide what was happening. A voice came clearly through the fresh morning air as the Mandan thrust his lance into the ground. ''Hear me, Father of us all!'' He now raised an elaborately decorated ceremonial peace pipe toward the sun. ''You, the Father of the sun which gives us light and warmth, you the sun which has the medicine to start fires. Listen to me, the speaker for the Mandan, and grant me your favor. I wish you through my right finger to set my shield afire!'' Lone Wolf had a small magnifying glass in his right hand. He had adjusted the glass so that only a pinpoint of the sun's rays shone on the shield while he spoke. In a matter of seconds, smoke began to rise from the leather shield, and the Blackfeet observed this with awe. Then the shield burst into flames and Lone Wolf cast it upon the ground, and reined his horse toward the bushes. His horse walked slowly until it could not be seen any more by the Blackfeet.

''Oh mighty One,'' came Lone Wolf's loud voice. ''Make my horse grow.''

Murmurs could be heard from the Blackfeet as Lone Wolf rode out of the bushes on the huge Clydesdale.

''Now grant me one more favor, oh mighty One,'' Lone Wolf continued. ''Grant that my people's coup sticks will make thunder and bring death to our attackers.''

The Mandan's War Society now marched out from behind the wall, each carrying a coup stick which cleverly camouflaged a Sharpes rifle. Lone Wolf rode slowly to the men, raised both hands toward the sun, hands which held tobacco. ''Oh mighty Father, I give you tobacco for this favor."

The War Society now raised their coup sticks toward the Blackfeet, many of whom had exposed their positions as they watched, entranced by the proceedings taking place before them. The Sharpes rifles roared and many Blackfeet fell, dead or wounded. When they had recovered from the shock of the magic, they gathered their dead and wounded and melted into the woods, finally disappearing over the treeless hill behind the woods.

The Mandans watched as the Blackfeet slowly disappeared into the distance. It was on this day that the Blackfeet gave Lone Wolf a new name, "Many Horses in One," and his own people began to call him this.

CHAPTER V

The first winter after the rifles were acquired, a buffalo hunt was organized, for the warriors were eager to try the new weapons. As the civil chief explained to Thor and Sam, in the old days before they had had horses, the buffalo were much more difficult to kill. Sometimes they would follow the wolves and if they were fortunate enough to bring down a buffalo, they were chased away and the Indians took the meat. Other times the buffalo were chased over a cliff. The old medicine men had a stone about the size of a man's fist which they claimed could speak to the buffalo. If their prey heard the call of the stone, the herd could be enticed in the direction of the cliff and once near the cliff, the Indians would get behind the herd, stampeding it over the edge.

Only the more surefooted horses were kept for the buffalo hunt, and it was these favorite mounts which were kept in the lodges during severe weather. Before a hunt, these horses were painted with symbols and bright cloth was braided into their manes and tails.

The honor of locating the herd was given this time to Thor Elkinson, and when he had done this, temporary tipis were erected and all readied themselves for the kill. Not all of the warriors had rifles and these hunters checked their lances and bows and arrows. While these preparations were progressing, some of the women were cutting stakes which they would drive through the hides to secure them to the ground. Other women preferred building square frames on which to lace the hides.

Some of the young men hoped to have visions the night before the great hunt, visions foretelling the brave deeds they would perform the following day. Being young and showing outstanding courage could bring a young warrior fame, wealth, and entrance into one of the tribal societies to which he aspired.

To live a long life was not the way of the Indian. He hoped to live a short life but an heroic one so that his deeds would be talked about at the campfires in the years to come. Who would want to live to be so old that you had no teeth, so old that the squaws had to chew your food for you until it was tender enough for your gums? Then later, if you lived to be very old, you would be left to sit in a cave or a tipi abandoned after a hunt and sing the death chant, not taking any food until death overcame you, your body then being food for the wolves.

The light was just beginning to show in the east when the men mounted their horses and moved silently toward the herd. Some of them carried the old buffalo stone which their ancient ancestors had carried and they smiled at themselves for their behavior. No one spoke, but used sign language to communicate, for voices could spook the herd and it might be long before another chance so good would come.

Thor, in the lead, raised his hand as a signal to stop. Next, he pointed ahead and put both hands to his ears, thumbs extended outward and his index fingers extended upward and slightly bent toward the back of his head, the sign for buffalo.

In half an hour, the kill had been made and the herd had stampeded out of sight, but not out of hearing, for the earth trembled as the great beasts lumbered on and on. It was not unusual for there to be fifty thousand in one herd, and one could ride all day and not see the end. If one of the really large herds stampeded, the sound could be heard and their passing could be felt for great distances and the dust kicked up could become clouds which could be seen for miles.

The women became busy at their skinning and occasionally one would gut the buffalo and sink her teeth into the warm, raw liver, a great delicacy. When it was finished, meat dried, hides prepared and the travois loaded to transport the harvest, all that was left were a few bones and some of those had been taken to be used for needles and other implements, such as hoes.

Back in the village everything was stored away and most of the people went for a well deserved swim. The Mandans were a clean people, much more so than many of the whites who settled later in the Rockies. The Mandan took a bath in the river at least once a day and on this day some of them took steam baths. Their steam bathhouses were small, the steam generated from hot stones which were placed in water. After the steam bath, the occupants usually ran to the edge of the river and dived into it.

———————

Five years had passed quickly, it seemed to Sam. He had gone with Thor on several different trapping expeditions. At twenty-one, he had grown into a fine, strong young man, standing six-feet four inches and weighing well over two hundred pounds, with a grace of movement seldom seen in a man so large. He was one in a century, if one believed Thor, who had watched him grow and had taught him his trade.

Sam hardly ever missed with the rifle or pistol and his agility with throwing the knife or tomahawk amazed Thor more as each day passed. His hearing and sense of smell were of the best plus ten, Thor said. Thor had been a good teacher and example and Sam had that trait of a good student, a great interest in the subject. The Indians too, were proud of Sam, proud to claim him as their own.

Sam had learned the ways of the Indian, and combined these ways with the ways of the white man, using this knowledge to out-figure Indians, white men, or animal life. Sam was not a cruel man, but a compassionate one, a trait which brought him great respect from the Indians as well as the few white men he met while with Thor. His reputation as a trapper and hunter had spread throughout the mountain area and would eventually be brought to the attention of the writers east of the Mississippi River. His reputation would not be believed by many who said that no one man could possibly possess all of these traits.

Sam had adopted the Mandans as his people. He held a privileged seat at all council meetings and his wisdom was listened to with eagerness. He repeatedly refused to accept the combined civil, war, and ceremonial chief's role which no other Mandan had ever held. Then one day, the tribe, in a special meeting, presented him with a new symbol and name. The combined leadership of the Mandan had made and presented to Sam at this meeting, a round, fur hat, colored bright red, and after the presentation a law was passed that no one else could ever wear or have such a hat. Sam from this meeting forward was to be known as Son of Manitou. The women of the village constructed a lodge suitable for Son of Manitou not far from the one occupied by Many Horses in One and his mother, Beaver Pelt.

Four hardwood poles about ten feet in length were cut, leaving a fork at the top. Then a circle of ground was dug out about fifty feet in diameter three feet deep, with a dirt ramp left where the door would be. The four poles were placed in holes prepared for that purpose and four stout horizontal logs were placed into the forks at the top of the poles. Small logs were laid side by side at a forty-five degree angle from the ground to the four horizontal logs. From the horizontal logs to the top of the lodge, other small poles were laid side by side at about a twenty-five degree angle. A hole was left at the top of the lodge to permit campfire smoke to escape. The small, round canoes of the Mandan, when not in use, sat on top of the lodges, to be used over the smoke hole when it rained. On top of these logs and laid in the opposite direction were tied small willow branches and over these was placed sod.

In these lodges were placed the valuables of the owners, sometimes even including their prize horses. If need be, the lodge could accommodate twenty-five to thirty people. The Mandan lodge was the best insulated of all and only modern man has found better means of insulation. The white man recognized the desirable traits of these lodges and copied them, building the sod houses.

CHAPTER VI

N ot long after his twenty-first birthday, Sam, Son of Manitou, waved to his friends as he trotted his horse out of the village, followed by two pack horses. He could feel the autumn chill in the air as well as see the haze which softened the hillsides around him. It was September and one could feel the coming of winter in the cool, easterly breeze.

"A man needs solitude once in a while, a time to think, a time to dream," he had told Thor and Many Horses in One.

He rode westward, toward the high Rockies. In his pack he carried a few extra pairs of moccasins which Beaver Pelt had made for him and some buffalo jerky. His clothing was made entirely of animal skins and his leggings were fur lined. His pistol and knife were carried at his belt and his rifle was covered with a decorated, fringed scabbard to protect it from the dust, rain, and snow. On his head he wore his pride and joy, the red fur hat, symbol of the Son of Manitou.

That first night Sam made camp by a small river. There wasn't much water in it now, but the wide river bed told how much water it could carry during the spring runoff or after a flash flood.

Sam leaned against a tree trunk as he whittled on a piece of wood. Pipe in mouth, he enjoyed the solitude and listened to the water as it flowed around a boulder in the stream. He removed his pipe, laid it near the fire, sheathed his knife and from his pouch took a mouth organ and began to play it as he looked up at the full moon and the tall trees surrounding him.

"Thank you God, for such beauty," he said softly as he looked up at the heavens.

The fire was almost out as Sam moved away into the trees and prepared for sleep, covering himself with his buffalo robe and adjusting his rifle by his side.

He was awakened by a sense of danger. He didn't move, but slowly turned his head toward the horses, whose ears were up and whose heads were turned toward the south. They didn't seem very nervous, so Sam concluded that whatever the danger, it was not nearby. He threw back the robe and rose to his feet, sniffing the air, but could detect no strange odor. Next he picked a leaf from a nearby bush and tossed it into the air to see if he was up or downwind from whatever it was. The leaf slowly drifted to the ground behind him and he told himself, good, I'm downwind.

He walked over to his horse and saddled him. He picked up his rifle, mounted, and rode to the river bank.

Carefully, he examined the banks of the river, and seeing nothing suspicious, he urged Buck into the water and splashed across the knee deep river. He went slowly, watching for signs and after riding perhaps a quarter of a mile, he saw the first unusual sign, a broken twig at the end of a small tree limb. He dismounted and examined the ground beneath the limb and found horse tracks, lots of them.

Couldn't have been more than half an hour ago or not more than an hour, he told himself. Looked like a big war party, maybe thirty warriors. So that was what he had sensed. He'd been lucky he hadn't camped any nearer the trail or he might have crossed over before he was ready! As he rode back toward his camp, he spoke to his horse, "Buck, this war party could bring us trouble yet, more than we've bargained for, too, you old biscuit eater." He leaned forward and patted Buck on the neck.

Four days later he crossed the tracks of that same war party. He dismounted and inspected the tracks once more and decided they were only a few hours old. He had hoped to have put more distance between them and himself when he stayed an extra day at one camp.

They're headed north, maybe going home, and whatever they'd come south for, it was for no good, he thought.

The following day about noon, as he reached the top of a small hill, he could see buzzards circling in the sky a few miles ahead. He pushed his horses into a long lope and when he had circled the base of a large hill, he could see what the buzzards had been watching. Five conestoga wagons lined in a row. The poor devils didn't know what hit them, Sam thought. All of the horses were gone, the wagons had been looted and dead bodies were everywhere.

Sam dismounted and tied his horses. He walked through the carnage and found that the only one not scalped had been an infant boy, perhaps a year old, who had an arrow through his chest. Sam examined the arrow; Blackfeet, he whispered to himself.

He began to dig graves for the dead, using a shovel he'd found attached to the side of one of the wagons. How did they miss that? he wondered grimly. As he prepared to bury the first person, he heard a moan. He crouched and swung around, pulling his pistol as he did so. He saw no one, but the moan came again faintly, and his eyes searched for movement and then he saw an arm raise and drop. He holstered his pistol and ran to the youth who lay beneath the bodies of two men. He had an arrow in him, Sam saw, as he rolled the two dead men away. He was not scalped, for apparently the Indians hadn't noticed him under the two dead men. The arrow was in the boy's left shoulder and there appeared to have been only a small amount of bleeding. Sam tore the lad's shirt and inspected the wound. It could have been worse he thought. He held the arrow firmly and turned the boy on his side. He could see a lump under the skin on his back where the point had almost punctured the skin. He carefully cut the shaft of the arrow in two, then after fixing bandages near at hand, he pushed and worked the arrowhead out through the skin at the back of the lad's shoulder, then pulled the shaft of the arrow out, very carefully. The lad was still unconscious and Sam was glad, for he hoped to treat the wounds before he regained consciousness. He poured whiskey through the wounds, applied a salve which Beaver Pelt prescribed for such cases, and then bandaged them firmly. He then covered the boy and thinking that the less disturbance he had the better, Sam quietly resumed the grim business of burying the dead.

Quite a while afterward, the young man opened his eyes and saw, through his blurred vision, the image of a man laying wood on a fire. He attemped to sit up, but the pain in his shoulder prevented that and he spoke in a tired voice, "Who are you?"

Sam looked over at the youth and told him, "Don't try to move or you'll open your wounds. My name is Sam Sidwell. I found you lying under the bodies of two dead men."

"Did anyone else survive? My parents and brother and sister, are they all right?" He again tried to rise and once more fell back and lay there, fear for his family etched deeply in his pallid face.

"Now there, take it easy," Sam told him as he knelt beside

the boy. "I buried twenty-nine people . . . how many were there in your party?"

The boy looked up at the sky as he counted to himself. "Thirty-two, there were thirty-two of us, though!"

"If there were thirty-two of you," Sam said as he rose, "then two are prisoners of the Blackfeet, or your count isn't right, or they ran off or something, because I only buried twenty-nine. What's your name?"

"Andrew," came the reply, "Andrew Fredericks."

"What were you doing out here with only five wagons?" Sam asked.

"We were headed for Fort Bridger from Independence, Missouri, and we hoped we could stay near or at Fort Bridger for the winter, then in the spring go on with a longer wagon train to Oregon, to settle in the Willamette Valley. We followed the North Platte River until we reached the South Platte and we left it three days back. We were on the South Pass route, weren't we? What am I saying? What difference does it make now? My whole family must be dead, Mr. Sidwell." He grew more agitated and tried to sit up once more, but again the pain and weakness overcame him and he sank back.

Sam laid his hand on the boy's good shoulder and tried to reassure him, saying "Sam will be fine, Andrew, just call me Sam, and just as soon as you're ready to ride, we'll take up the trail of the Blackfeet to see if we can't find out about prisoners. How old are your brother and sister? If they were younger than you, then the Blackfeet may have them. They haven't taken many grown folks prisoner since they grew to hate the white man after Meriwether Lewis and one of his men killed two of them in self defense."

As Andrew described his younger brother and slightly older sister, Sam reassured him that he couldn't recall anyone bearing those descriptions among the dead, though he thought to himself that some of them had been pretty badly mutliated. No sense in telling the lad that, he reasoned. Or that being a prisoner of the Blackfeet couldn't be considered fortunate, for the lad felt bad enough already.

Sam prevailed upon Andrew to wait a few days before starting after the war party. "You're not going to do any good if you don't have time to heal a little. We'll cover more ground a lot faster if you're able to keep a good steady trot. A horse and rider can cover a lot of territory in a day's time like that, but you can't be too sore or you'll never last."

Andrew knew the big man was right and knew from his matter-of-fact manner that he would be equal to finding the Blackfeet and releasing their prisoners if anyone could. He did as Sam ordered, eating and sleeping, doing everything he could to regain his strength, and at the end of the third day, Sam pronounced the wounds healing well enough to start out the following morning.

Andrew felt giddy as he dressed and pulled on his boots, but after breakfast he felt strong enough to help Sam as he struck camp. Sam had mended an old saddle which the Indians hadn't taken and with this, he saddled the easiest riding of the pack horses, a small sorrel with a roman nose, called Freckles because of his speckled face. Freckles wasn't much to look at, but he was willing and the easiest of the two to do without. The big roan, his partner, could carry the packs until they found another horse. The packing finished, they mounted and rode at a walk at first to see how Andrew stood up to it. After a while, when they had crossed a sparkling stream and begun to climb higher into the hills, they alternated the walk with a trot now and then. The trail wasn't hard to follow, for the days had been sunny and still and the tracks looked almost fresh. The foothills gave way to mountains, however, and the trail became dimmer, harder to follow. One afternoon it vanished altogether, and Sam told Andrew to find fresh game while he scouted for the trail. When he came back to the small mountain meadow, he found Andrew turning a turkey over the fire.

"Now that's more like it," Sam grinned. "That venison jerky can get old after awhile!"

He had picked up the trail farther around the mountain where the hooves of the Indian ponies had hit softer ground. He had followed it until he had seen it lead down out of the mountains, apparently to cross a wide valley, then had turned and ridden back to Andrew. It was getting late, so they'd camp and start early in the morning.

They were on their way before dawn, for Sam wanted to get across that valley as early as possible. There was very little cover, and how far ahead the Indian village might be, he didn't know. Accordingly, they held to a steady trot, avoiding bare ground as much as possible, for stirring up any dust would be a dead giveaway. Fortunately, that wasn't too difficult, for the grass was stirrup high in most places. Good rangeland, Sam thought to himself.

The tracks lay in a straight line across the valley and they picked them up on the other side of a stream. Sam dismounted and again examined the tracks which paralleled the stream, "We're close, Andrew."

"How close?" Andrew asked as he bent from the saddle.

"Half a day or less," Sam replied as he checked the tracks once more.

"How can you tell if this is the war party we're after?"

"See those tracks?" Sam pointed, "Those horses are shod; Indian ponies go barefoot and those tracks have been with us right along. From now on, Andrew, no talking, no sound of any kind. You understand?"

"Yes."

It was an hour later when Sam raised his hand and stopped and pointed, "There, across the shallow end of the lake, is their village."

Tepees could be seen scattered along the shore of the lake and beyond, in the trees. Sam and Andrew had reined in their horses before they reached the edge of the willows which bordered the stream they had been following.

"There's a whole parcel of them alright, and they feel they are in no danger."

"How can you know that?"

"They have posted no sentries. That will help some, and we're downwind of them, also. Now do you understand why we saturated all of our belongings with the smoke last night? Our human scent has been replaced by that of the smoke of the cedar wood. You laughed when I told you to remove your boots and socks to smoke them also, but foot odor is the strongest odor. I can tell from which tribe an Indian is just from smelling his moccasin print. Andrew, this will be our plan. I will make some stilts and at sunup, I will be out into the lake, maybe thirty or forty feet from shore and the stilts will be holding me so it will appear that I'm standing on the water. When they see me, all of them I hope, will come to the shoreline. I will take a few steps which will appear to them as though I am walking on the water. While they are watching me, you will try to free the prisoners. After awhile, I will walk toward shore until I reach those rocks over there." Sam pointed as Andrew watched attentively.

"Then what?"

"By that time you will have freed the prisoners and be on your way over here. But now the problem, when the Indians realize that they have been tricked, they'll be all over us. How can we escape that many Blackfeet?" Sam mused as he studied the rocks. "What I think we'd better do is cut some willows, enough for all of us, and tie them together. When you have reached this side again, we'll wrap the willows around us as camouflage and blend into the other willows bordering the lake on this side. We'll be counting on the Blackfeet being in such angry pursuit of us that they'll ride right past us, then we'll make our escape. First, we must take the horses up into the hills to hide them. By the time we get back and make our preparations, we won't have too long to wait.''

Early the next morning, a few Blackfeet were moving about, some probably still asleep, and others building cook fires when they heard a voice from across the lake.

''Him standing on the water,'' one Blackfoot shouted as he pointed. Sam now took three big steps to hold their attention and all the time he talked to Manitou. More Indians were drawn to the water's edge and their murmurs could be heard by Sam across the lake as they informed the newcomers of the phenomenon.

Andrew had located the prisoners, both tied to a tree and left unguarded. He was overjoyed to find his sister, Carolyn, and brother, Arthur. Thank God they were alive! They saw him spring from behind the nearby bushes and in a second their thongs were cut and he had motioned to them to follow him as he put his finger to his lips and started into the trees.

Carolyn grabbed his arm and pointed to a tree not far away to which a young Indian boy was tied. Andrew ran forward, cut his bonds, and they all disappeared into the woods.

Sam kept his act going long enough for them to reach the spot where they'd hidden the willow branches, before he walked behind the rocks and ran silently to where the young people were frantically wrapping themselves into the woven branches. It was done, and they were still as the Indians streamed around the lake past the rocks and took the trail which Sam and Andrew had made the day before as they rode into the hills to hide the horses. Now Andrew could see how important it had been to ride so far up the stream after they had left so obvious a trail at the beginning. It should take the Blackfeet a long time to pick up their trail, whereas they could cut directly across the hills to reach their mounts.

They reached their horses and Sam told Andrew to double up with the Indian boy while Carolyn and Arthur rode the roan. Riding double would be slow going, but it couldn't be helped.

''Let's move,'' Sam told them when all were ready. They headed for the high country and after two hours it began to rain. Sam smiled as he told them, ''This will destroy our tracks, and if we're lucky we've seen the last of them. If they're really persistent though, they may keep looking until they find our tracks once it's stopped raining."

The Indian boy spoke up, "My people, the Miniconjou, should be coming back from a buffalo kill. They've been gone many days and they always camp at Blue Water Creek on their way back to our village. Blue Water Creek is over those mountains." He pointed to mountains off to the south.

"That beats just running; let's give it a try," Sam decided. He reined his horse in that direction, and the others kept close behind him as he rode at a brisk trot toward the distant mountains.

Carolyn Fredricks glanced back at her brother as they trotted, to see how he was doing. He held her around the waist and bounced slightly, for the big roan had a hard trot. He grinned however, to show her he was game.

"Those Indians will never take us captive again," she told her brother as she urged her horse up beside Sam's.

Sam smiled at her sympathetically as he answered her unspoken thoughts, "Don't worry, I think the worst is over for you, Miss Carolyn. You've been lucky, the three of you, when you think of what happened to the rest of your party." He glanced at her, realizing that her parents were part of that party. Her eyes shone with unshed tears and then she looked away.

Sam gave her time to recover as he told of how he had found Andrew when he reached the wagon train. "He's got plenty of grit, that one," Sam told his sister, "just as his younger brother, here!"

He turned back to Carolyn and asked, "Did you hear what they planned to do with you?"

"Something about the Crow, making a trade with them," replied Carolyn. "Do they do that sometimes?"

"Sometimes," Sam replied. He knew what happened when the Crow got hold of prisoners, but kept it to himself. Sometimes the Blackfeet ransomed prisoners to the Crow, and the Crow women, in particular, delighted in dancing around their prisoners, hacking at them with their knives, and spitting in their faces, before they really got down to business, business these young people didn't need to hear about.

He clucked to his horse, "Come along, old Buck, let's stir your hocks up a little faster," as he thought to himself, these kids are too young to die that way.

They kept up a tireless pace on the long, steady climb, the boys walking beside the horses on the steeper portions of the climb. When they had reached the summit, the Indian boy said, "Look over there!"

All looked toward where he was pointing. Way down among the trees, on the floor of the valley far below could be seen many Indians, some pulling travois and others riding with an Indian walking along side. These Indians had probably lost their horses in the hunt, and by holding to a stirrup could walk or trot beside a rider. However, most of them were mounted and leading a horse which pulled a travois loaded with buffalo jerky and hides.

"Quite a sight," Sam said, "smart, too, for they have scouts out."

As he spoke, they noticed one of the scouts dashing back to the main party at full speed. They were too far away for Sam to be able to tell whether they were looking up at them or saw something else, but he hoped they had been spotted.

"Let's move," he said, "there below us is our salvation."

"Look," Andrew pointed up the valley. "That's why the scout was high tailing it so fast."

"Blackfeet," commented Sam, "and I'll bet it's the ones looking for us."

The little party rapidly descended the side of the mountain, angling so that they would be behind the hunters and away from the Blackfeet.

"Let the Indian boy lead us to his people," Sam yelled as they neared the bottom, "there's less chance of a misunderstanding that way."

The Indian boy, with Andrew riding behind him, took the lead and as he rode to the front, he yelled at his horse and gave him his head, and the others streamed out behind him as fast as the rough ground of the valley floor permitted. They could see the faces of the hunting party clearly now as they watched them approach, then turned to also watch the Blackfeet who were stationed on a slight rise down the valley. The Blackfeet seemed to be uncertain about what to do next and hesitated. But Sam and his little troop were not uncertain and Carolyn told Arthur, "Hang on, we're going to make it all right!"

The three horses with their riders galloped into the Indian caravan amidst much commotion and preparation for the fight which they expected with the Blackfeet. Women were hurrying the children into the center of the caravan, "Time is short and we need to give the warriors room to prepare."

The young Indian boy led his small group past many surprised and puzzled people of his tribe as he sought out his father, Grey

Eagle.

"He's in the lead," shouted a brave in answer to the boy as he rode by him.

Grey Eagle was issuing orders when he spotted his son, Little Hawk dashing toward him. A short, happy reunion took place as Little Hawk introduced his companions.

"Hook-ah-hay," (welcome) Grey Eagle spoke as his horse pranced in a circle.

"Chief, I have an idea," Sam yelled.

In deference to the man who had saved his son, Grey Eagle called a council on the spot as they sat their horses. When the warriors had gathered, Grey Eagle turned to Sam and said, "Speak, friend of Little Hawk."

Sam's plan was quickly related to the men gathered there. "Have three rows of braves, the first in a sitting position, the second in a kneeling position, and the third standing directly behind those kneeling. When the Blackfeet charge us, each row in turn will shoot their arrows so that a constant hail of arrows will fall into the ranks of the galloping Blackfeet. The remainder of the Miniconjou can be ready to charge into the confused ranks of Blackfeet."

Grey Eagle approved of the stranger's plan and gave orders to that effect. In a short time all were ready. The young Miniconjou warriors were itching for a fight and had to be warned not to break rank or otherwise take on the Blackfeet in single combat.

Sam spotted a Blackfoot warrior giving orders to his men. He wore two eagle feathers in his hair. Only if he had taken twenty scalps could he wear even one feather, and this brave wore two. Sam looked at him with cold hatred in his eyes, thinking that he had killed the poor defenseless farmers of the wagon train.

"I wish to lead the horse warriors,' he told Grey Eagle.

Grey Eagle nodded and gave the command for fifteen mounted braves to follow Sam. Sam checked his bowie, pistol, and then stuck another pistol under his belt. He checked his Sharpes and motioned to the warriors to line up behind the archers.

Suddenly a bloodcurdling yell came from the Blackfeet as they streamed down the valley, straight at the Miniconjou. At around one hundred yards, Grey Eagle gave the order for his braves to commence firing. The Blackfeet were slowed by the first round of arrows and then thrown into confusion by the continuous hail of arrows. They continued for perhaps fifty or sixty yards through the murderous fire, struggling through fallen horses and men until the order was given to retreat.

"Now!" Sam shouted at his warriors and spurred his horse at the disordered, ragged ranks of the Blackfeet. The Miniconjous needed little encouragement however, and in seconds they were among their old enemies, hacking away with tomahawks or jabbing with their lances, some even left their horses to jump their enemies, uttering horrible screeches as they plunged their knives into the Blackfeet.

It was over within minutes as the few remaining Blackfeet melted into a stand of aspens toward the upper end of the valley. Sam saw those eagle feathers disappear behind a tree and he spurred his horse after him, rifle waving in his hand, and uttering his mountain man yell of revenge. The Miniconjou looked on in awe at the fury of the big fair haired mountain man.

Back in the middle of the caravan, Andrew saw Sam galloping toward the trees and tried to follow, but his older sister grabbed his rein. "Leave him alone, Andrew," she cautioned, "he knows what he's doing and you'd only make it more difficult," she added.

"But they are the ones who killed ma and pa, and it's my duty to make them pay," Andrew cried.

"Sam will make them pay, Andrew. Do as I say."

"All right, Carolyn," Andrew replied as he stared into the trees where Sam had dispppeared.

Suddenly they heard a blood curdling yell echoing off the mountain side. It sent a chill through Carolyn and her brothers and Carolyn said softly, "They paid, Andrew; Sam saw to that."

Sam had caught up with the retreating Indians when the brave who wore two feathers suddenly whirled his horse and jumped to the ground, knife in hand. Sam slid Buck to a stop and was running forward to meet the enemy even as his moccasined feet hit the dirt.

"You've got it, you sorry so and so," he yelled as he ran into the Indian at full speed. The Indian's knife struck Sam a glancing blow in the upper chest as he was thrown to the ground by the weight and force of Sam's body. It was then that Sam uttered his fierce cry as he plunged his bowie into the chest of the Blackfoot, extracted it, and took his enemy's scalp with one swift swipe of his knife. The four remaining Blackfeet who had halted at a distance, had seen enough and with one accord disappeared into the trees at a gallop.

Carolyn saw Sam first as he walked his horse back toward the Miniconjous and it was she who first saw that he was hurt. She ran to him as he dismounted. His left arm hung limp. What got into her she didn't know, but she hugged him as she said, "Thank God you're alive." Then she covered her confusion by fussing at him about getting hurt, telling him to let her examine his wound.

"Let's look at that shoulder," she ordered, "do you have anything for bandages?"

"Not much," drawled Sam, "we cached our supplies back before we got you away from the Blackfeet. Didn't have any way to pack supplies and you, too. I'm not hurt much anyway."

Little Hawk rode up and told Sam to follow him, and he led him to his mother. She signed for him to sit down so that she could examine his shoulder. She then proceeded to wash, dress, and bandage his shoulder deftly while Carolyn and her brothers watched.

That night the Miniconjous talked about their feats around the campfires and another, smaller group sat near a fire talking about the future.

"What is to become of us, Carolyn?" Andrew stared into the fire and continued, "We're a long way from home and in the middle of Indian country and this mountain wilderness."

Sam sat motionless, his knees drawn up and his right forearm rested across his right knee. He was staring into the crackling flames, his eyes unblinking, his thoughts far away. He hadn't heard a word the others had said, until Arthur jumped up and ran to his side and said, "I'll bet Sam has a plan, don't you Sam?"

"I was thinking," Sam said slowly as they all leaned forward, "that if we spent a few winters trapping, with fair luck we could make enough to give you three a fresh start. Another team and wagon and you could be on your way to wherever you wished. What do you say?"

The three answered in a chorus of agreement, excitement written on their faces. But Andrew voiced his reservations about Carolyn doing something like that. "Maybe we'd better go to Fort Bridger to see about finding a train for her to go ahead on," he suggested reluctantly.

"Oh no you don't, little brother," Carolyn broke in indignantly, "we're not going to be separated. I can stand anything you and Arthur can stand, and I'm not going to miss this. Why, how many girls ever get a chance like this?"

Andrew grinned at his sister, "Well now, it looks as though your tomboy ways are going to pay off, sis. At least you have the right things to wear to ride which is more than the other girls on the wagon train had." He thought back to the arguments Carolyn had presented to persuade her parents to let her ride from

Independence, to let her ride with her brothers instead of in the wagon as other girls usually did.

Carolyn was a tall girl, slender and lithe. She wore her dark, wavy hair in one long braid down her back. She was clad in a dark brown divided skirt so that she could ride astride. A heavy wool shirt and a short jacket to match her skirt made up her sensible attire. Her hat had been lost in the capture by the Blackfeet and her tannned face and sparkling brown eyes belied the fact of the experiences which she and Arthur had endured. Her spirits had not been broken by the experiences although she and her brothers had not yet fully comprehended the loss of their parents, so suddenly had everything happened.

The Fredricks' farm had been sold back in Derry, New Hampshire for now that the grandparents had died, the old farm had been sold to divide the proceeds among several children and Carolyn's parents had decided to use their share to go to Oregon to homestead. Besides, their father pointed out, the area they lived in near Derry was getting crowded and he wanted more room to breathe and a larger farm. Well, it hadn't worked out for him and their mother, but God willing, it might still do so for their children, Carolyn mused sadly. If we had only stayed in New Hampshire, they would still be alive, and since they were doing it largely on our account, we've got to manage so they didn't die in vain. I'm sure if we all stay together and work hard, we can make it somehow.

She looked away from the fire and into the faces of her brothers which also looked subdued, quiet, as no doubt they too, were thinking of their parents, their so good, self-sacrificing mother and father with their grand plans and ready humor. We'll try to live up to your dreams and example, she promised them silently.

"Well, let's make a stab at it, little brothers," she said.

She was vowing to take the place of their parents as far as possible, to encourage and stand by her brothers through thick and thin. It looked pretty thin right now, certainly.

Andrew and Arthur knew that their sister was trying to buck them up, to help them through this loss of their parents, and they loved her for it. They both spoke at once, "We'll do it, sis, with Sam to help us!"

They both went around the fire to hug their sister and then shook hands with Sam, too, and told him they'd try to do their share, they'd try not to be a burden on him.

Sam shook his head a little to quell the tears which had risen to his eyes while he watched the three young people. They were fine, brave, decent young people, he had told himself as he watched them and he'd sure try his hardest to see that nothing happened to them, or die trying!   '

CHAPTER VII

T wo days after the battle with the Blackfeet, Sam and his young troop rode back up the mountainside and this time each had a mount. The chief had presented Sam with three fine ponies in gratitude for the rescue of his young son, Little Hawk.

Carolyn's small horse was a sorrel with a blaze face and two white socks in back. Andrew's was a little larger and was an Appaloosa, a good tough breed. Arthur's pony was a paint, with black and white splotches distributed over his body and it would have been hard to tell whether he was predominantly white or black if it hadn't been for his black legs. They were very proud of their new mounts, for the Blackfeet had stolen the ones they'd ridden from Independence, Missouri.

They first rode back to where Sam had cached his supplies and there they camped. The following morning, the two pack horses were once more loaded with the tools, traps, and other supplies making up Sam's gear.

Then they had ridden back to the scene of the massacre so that the two boys and their sister could pay their respects to their dead. It had been a cold, dreary day as they rode to the scene of the carnage, and Sam's heart went out to the three young people as they knelt beside the graves. There was no way to tell which of them held their parents, but they felt as though they could communicate with them anyway as they each said a silent prayer while Sam held the horses a short distance away.

Sam looked away, for the sight of the three young people kneeling in a half circle saying their prayers for their parents brought back the death of old Andy Jackson and before that, the death of his own parents. We all have sad periods in our lives, he thought, and I'll do my best to help these kids through theirs. Before too long a large part of their memories will be happy ones as they remember the good times they had and the things they did together.

The air had a definite chill in it as they rode toward the headwaters of the Green River. Finally, one day, Sam pointed down from the hillside where they sat their horses toward a small creek which wound through the valley below.

"The headwaters of the Green River," he said as he leaned on his saddle horn. "This will be a good spot, plenty of water, grass, and protection from the winds. The creek has fish and the forest on either side of the creek has all kinds of wild berries, I'll be bound, from blueberries and blackberries to chokecherries.

"Due south about two hundred miles is Fort Bridger, on Black's Fork, and Fort Hall is about two hundred miles west of here, so we'll have two good places to sell our trappin's. The Oregon Trail crosses the Green River south of us and then goes on to Fort Bridger. That gives you some idea of where you are. Now we'd better skidaddle on down and set up a camp until we can get a cabin up; it won't be long before the snow flies."

They set up camp not far from the creek and over the fire that night, Sam became serious as he educated the three Fredericks to the dangers that were everywhere about them.

"Tomorrow," he told them, "you'll begin to learn how to use your weapons, and you'll practice every day until I think you're good enough to come out alive if you get in a tight spot. Out here, there's no one to depend on but yourself so you learn fast or else."

They were awakened at sunup by Sam's calling them to breakfast and after a hasty one, they set to at the serious business of getting their cabin built. The creek had slivers of ice along its bank and the hot coffee had really tasted good that morning. Winter came swiftly in the mountains.

At the end of the first month, Sam was pleased at the proficiency of his students in knife and tomahawk throwing. Each day some time had been set aside to practice as the work progressed on the cabin. Now the cabin was finished and the rough walls and rock fireplace were not unpleasing to the eye. Carolyn had a corner to herself where she could hang blankets for privacy and each had a bunk built into the cabin walls. Andrew and Arthur constructed some benches and a table while Sam prepared the traps.

The young people had taken to the life as if born to it and Sam was especially proud of young Andrew's ability to draw and fire his pistol with remarkable accuracy. Although he cautioned them all that practicing was a lot different from actually having to defend oneself. Then it took cold nerve and a willingness to kill, if need be, in self-defense.

Sam taught them how to set beaver traps and where. The traps had to be staked at the bottom of the shallow part of the ponds the beavers made by damming the creeks and small rivers. Scent had to be left near the trap to attract the beaver. When the beaver was caught, he drowned because the trap was staked below the water level.

As the pelts began to mount up, Carolyn asked how much a beaver pelt would bring.

"Four packs of good pelts could bring as much as seven hundred dollars," Sam said. "Each pack must have eighty hides. It takes one hundred and twenty fox hides to make a pack and ten buffalo hides make up a pack."

"How many bear hides make up a pack?" Carolyn asked.

"I'm not sure about bear. I've never hunted bear . . . if we decide to go after him, we'd better put at least fifteen to a pack and tell Jim Bridger or whomever we deal with what we have to a pack. If we go after bear, we sure don't want to fool with the grizzly; he's bad medicine. I want all of us to finish this up, not just some of us. Those grizz could put us under."

CHAPTER VIII

I n the eighteen months since the massacre of the wagon train, Arthur had grown taller; darker than his brother and sister, he had an olive complexion, hazel eyes, and darker hair. He was still of medium height, but compact, well coordinated and his prowess with the tomahawk was unique. He was fun-loving and was always teasing his sister.

Carolyn had become even prettier, with a warm glow of tanned cheeks and her dark eyes and hair fairly shone with good health. She and her brothers had progressed to buckskin clothing as their own had worn out and Carolyn wore a buckskin skirt which came to below her knees and high moccasins which protected her legs to the knees. An overblouse of buckskin which she wore with either skirt or buckskin pants completed her clothing.

Andrew was the thin, wiry one he'd always been, but though thin, his muscles were like whipcord, and the outdoor living had been beneficial for all of them.

As for Sam, he was in the very prime of his young manhood. Strong, stalwart, he made as fine a figure of a man as anyone could want. Quiet, but with a dry sense of humor, Sam had the attributes of a strong man, gentle, but firm when necessary. He could spring into action in a split second, fast thinking and moving, and deadly. Calm and deliberate when ordinary circumstances prevailed. His blue eyes, fair hair, and freckled complexion gave him an engaging look which belied his training and experience.

Sam was twenty-three now; Carolyn, twenty-one; Andrew, eighteen; and Arthur, sixteen. Sam had assumed the role of guardian to the boys, but Carolyn so near to his age, had proven more of a partner to Sam and had also worked hard to provide the solace and good cheer which her brothers needed after the deaths of their parents.

While her heart had been sore, too, she had kept herself busy in making the cabin as homelike as possible for her brothers and Sam. Sam fell under the spell of her womanly characteristics and admired her patience with them all and her skillful adoption of the life which they now lived. She sang, ran, and played with Arthur, and worked along with Andrew and Sam at whatever task lay before them. Thus they all worked together and sat around the fire in the evening, talking about their future plans, plans which more and more seemed to include all of them.

Sam's eyes followed Carolyn often as she moved about the cabin or clearing and he watched her with a new light in his eyes.

She in turn became more aware of the tall young man who had been such a good friend. Hitherto, she had teased Sam along with her brothers, but suddenly a constraint seemed to have come between them as they grew increasingly conscious of each other.

One day as they rode their trapline, while the others checked the beaver traps, she asked Sam what he'd thought of doing if they went on to Oregon. Had he considered coming with them?

"I'd been sorta planning on heading south," Sam said hesitantly. "But do you really want to go on to Oregon? Do you think you might consider coming to New Mexico or Texas with me? We're pretty good partners, the four of us, and maybe we shouldn't break up a good team." He laid his hand over hers as it rested on her saddle horn. She colored and looked back at him with her level gaze. "But Sam, you need to be free to do as you wish with your life; you've been fine to us, but it's time you went about your own living. We'll be all right now." She glanced at him, wondering how he'd taken her little speech, hoping it hadn't sounded as halfhearted as it was.

"Why, don't you know how I feel about you?" He spoke softly, "For the first time I've felt right about things. You've given that feeling to me by being you; you're all that I've dreamed of in a woman, Carolyn. So thoughtful of your brothers, always cheerful whatever the circumstances, and we've had some pretty tough times to get through in the last eighteen months, haven't we?"

She grinned back at him, remembering, thinking of the difficulties she and her brothers had gotten themselves into. But always Sam had been there, coming to their rescue, quietly and patiently explaining and showing them the easier, best way to go about the life of a mountain trapper.

He had told Carolyn that he bet everyone in these mountains had heard of her by now. She was the only white woman living in the hills, and not only living there but doing the work of a man and doing it right well. She had taken Sam's compliment with quiet appreciation, but had dismissed it as nothing unusual. She only did what was necessary and what most women would have done in her place. As she thought back, her hand tightened unconsciously on Sam's and she wondered how she could live without him if he ever rode away from them.

"We've had good times, and scary ones, Sam, and you've made a man out of Andrew and Arthur is fast becoming one. He's more capable than most grown men back in the cities." She amended her statement, "At least at the kind of things we've been doing. Our father was certainly capable at farming and I guess there are different kinds of self-reliance so perhaps I shouldn't criticize city people. It seems to me they're missing a lot, though, Sam, and they'll probably never know it."

"It takes all kinds of people to make up the world, I suppose," replied Sam, "and you and your brothers are my kind." He went on with a look in his eyes which thrilled Carolyn, "Would you marry me, Carolyn? I can't face the thought of not seeing you every day, not to share our daily lives would be unthinkable . . . I love you, Carolyn, and I hope that you may feel the same way?"

Carolyn covered his hand with her other hand as she replied, "Sam I've loved you for a long time now, and being with you for the rest of my life, loving you, building a life together, would make me the happiest woman in the world!"

They leaned together for their first kiss, and then pulling apart, laughing, they dismounted and hugged each other for the sheer joy of sharing their love.

As they rode back to the cabin, they met Andrew riding out and he was surprised to see that they didn't have any pelts with them. "Nothing at all?"

Sam and Carolyn looked at one another sheepishly and laughed, then looked back at Andrew with their eyes dancing. "We have a surprise for you, Andrew," Carolyn said, glowing with happiness.

"I know, you and Sam are going to get married," broke in Andrew. "Arthur and I wondered if you'd ever find out what we've known for a long time!" He grinned and slapped Sam on the back and then gave Carolyn a brotherly hug.

"Think you can stand me as one of your family?" Sam asked.

"Hey, you made us part of your family first," retorted Andrew, "all you're doing is making it official."

They rode back to the cabin, anxious to break the news to Arthur who had stayed behind to start supper. When he was told, he beamed from ear to ear saying, "That's great, Sam, that's really great! You can't say you don't know what you're letting yourself in for, either!"

"Tonight we're going to have a council meeting and make plans, "Sam told him. "Carolyn and I have some ideas and we want your opinions."

That night after supper as they worked at various tasks before their fire, they discussed more fully what Carolyn and Sam had touched lightly upon earlier.

"At the end of this season which will be our second winter," Sam told the others, "we ought to have a pretty good stake, but after we take our pelts in maybe we ought to find another likely spot for one more season. We'll decide after we turn our pelts over and see how much we get for them."

"Anyway, what do you say to heading south to homestead, to start our own ranch somewhere in New Mexico Territory? We ought to be able to put together a good sized ranch which is what I'd like to do, and I think we'd all take to it. What do you say?"

Andrew spoke first and heartily in favor of the idea. "I'm ready now. Maybe we'll not need to trap another winter!"

Carolyn laughed and blushed as she told her brothers, "Sam and I thought we'd ride over to the Oregon Trail and see if one of the wagon trains doesn't have a minister to marry us, that is if you two think you can keep things going here all right?"

"Don't worry about a thing," chimed in Arthur, "we'll manage fine; gee, it's good to see you two so happy!"

The rest of that evening was spent planning for their move to the Southwest, where there was supposed to be good grazing land to be had.

A few days later, when Sam and Carolyn figured everything was caught up pretty well and there was nothing which her brothers couldn't handle, they saddled their horses and packed a pack horse, preparing to leave.

It was a cold, crisp morning, but clear, no sign of snow, although it wasn't too late in the season for it. Sam cautioned Andrew and Arthur to travel together along the trap line if it did begin to storm. The boys reassured them that they'd be careful and not to worry and waved, grinning, as Sam and Carolyn trotted out of the clearing leading the pack horse.

"What if we have to wait for the wagons a long time?" asked Carolyn as she turned in her saddle to wave, "Do you think they'll be all right?"

"The trains hit the trail as early as possible," said Sam, "so I reckon we ought to meet up with one of the earliest."

They sat their horses on a little rise as they watched a long wagon train winding snake-like toward them. The white canvas tops shone in the sunlight and seemed to reach the horizon. It was a big train, all right.

"Surely they'll have a preacher somewhere in that bunch of people," Carolyn said, breaking the silence.

By way of reply, Sam spurred Buck and uttering a yell, tore down the little hill toward the train, Carolyn in close pursuit. When they had ridden within a mile or so of the wagon train, they were met by two scouts, curious to talk with them.

Sam raised his hand and gave the Indian sign of friendship before they reached hailing distance. They rode back along the train, some of whose members wondered at the jubilant yell which was uttered by the tall mountain man as he learned that there was a preacher in the train. As a matter of fact, there were four that he knew of, the scout told them.

That evening in front of the camp fire of Mr. and Mrs. Jonathan Simmons, who were their witnesses, Sam and Carolyn were married. Afterward, as they shared the supper Mrs. Simmons had cooked, they answered questions put to them by not only the Simmons family, but by the wagon master who was eager to know of any dangers they might reasonably expect to encounter.

There were many glances cast toward the handsome young couple, so dashing in their buckskins, and looking so much at home in what the easterners felt to be so alien and dangerous an environment. They watched, marveling, as the young couple waved goodbye and rode off alone into the darkness, the wagon master calling good luck to them as he waved goodbye.

That night by the small campfire was to be a night never to be forgotten by Sam and Carolyn. Their love for one another blossomed as they told each other of their love and supposed that no one else had ever felt that way, the way they felt about each other.

As they were saddling their horses the following morning, Carolyn suddenly froze. Sam sensed it also as he listened, motionless. Neither moved, but stood quietly taking in all of the impressions which came to them. "Comanche," Carolyn whispered.

"Yes," Sam concurred.

"Not too far away, either, maybe less than a quarter of a mile?" Carolyn nodded in the direction which led up the valley.

"Let's put the leather mocs on the horses," Sam decided, "it will soften the hoofbeats."

"Right," Carolyn replied as she took hers from her saddlebag and bent to fasten them on her pony's feet.

Leaving the pack horse tied back in the brush, Sam said, "You take the east side of the river and I'll take the west, but don't take any chances."

They disappeared into the trees. Carolyn made contact with the Comanches first. Two were out away from the encampment, apparently looking for game when suddenly they found a squaw sitting a stationary horse right in front of them. Carolyn did nothing, said nothing, nor moved. She just sat there, studying the two braves. She had judged correctly, for the one on the right moved first. He apparently thought that he could overpower the squaw quickly, and she would be his before his companion made a move. It was only seconds before the second warrior made his move also. Carolyn threw her bowie and it sank deep in the chest of the first warrior. He slumped slowly to the ground as his hands embraced the hilt of the knife. The other sprang forward in fury, but too late, he fell with a tomahawk to the head which left nothing to be seen through the blood.

Carolyn continued to sit, again motionless, staring at the bodies of the two Comanches and listening. Then she dismounted and retrieved her weapons, remounted, and slowly, carefully, picked her way toward the Indian camp. As she drew nearer, she heard commotion and voices. She checked her Sharpes rifle as she dismounted and moved quickly through the underbrush until she was able to see movement in the camp. It was then she heard a shot, quickly followed by a second. The third shot was her own as she stood up, shouldered her rifle and fired at an Indian, who, knife in hand, was ready to strike at Sam who was wrestling with another warrior. Carolyn hit her target and the Indian fell forward face downward to the ground, his arms outstretched above his head. A moan was heard as Sam removed his bowie from his opponent's

stomach. He wiped the blood from his knife on the grass, and looked toward Carolyn who was walking toward him.

"Are you all right, honey?" He took her in his arms, holding
her close.

"You didn't want me to become a widow just as I became a
wife, did you?" She chuckled, even though she had paled under her
tan.

Sam looked down at her, saying in a low voice, "It would take
more than that to take me from you, my dear."

CHAPTER IX

"How much do you think this cow weighs?" Carolyn and Sam were skinning a cow elk which they'd hung from a tree not far from the cabin.

"Dressed out, maybe three hundred and fifty pounds," Sam estimated as he inspected the carcass.

"Andrew!" Sam called to him as he came from the cabin.

Andrew wiped his sleeve across his mouth as he told his sister, "Sis, those biscuits were sure good. What can I do for you, Sam?"

"Cut two forked limbs about five feet long, and bury them a couple of feet deep in the ground on each side of the fire," Sam told him as he motioned toward the fire he'd built earlier. "Then cut another limb to place in the forks so that your sister and I can hang the meat to dry. This should make good jerky. Where's Arthur?"

"He's just finishing breakfast; we've been giving the biscuits a fit," grinned Andrew.

"He can watch the meat once we have it hung," Sam said.

"I think we should make some pemmican," he told Carolyn as they worked on the elk, cutting it into long thin strips.

"I think so, too," Carolyn concurred. "When the jerky is thoroughly dried, I'll do that."

Pemmican was a combination of the jerky pounded to a powder with honey added sparingly and berries or other dried fruit added to the mixture. It was great to take when they were traveling, carried in the leather pouches the Indians called parfleches. It lasted a long time and was quite nourishing.

"We may have need of it on our trip to Fort Hall," Sam said.

Carolyn glanced at her husband inquiringly, "How soon do we leave?" Mounting excitement was in her voice.

"Guess as soon as we finish with this meat?" Sam grinned at her. "Since our furs need to be sold, there's no sense in waiting any longer. The sooner we know where we stand, money-wise, the better. We can either head south or start looking for another good trapping area, depending on what we decide?"

"Do you think we're getting in too big a hurry to go south?" Carolyn smiled up at Sam as he slipped an arm around her waist.

"There's no doubt but what we're eager," Sam smiled down at her, "but I think our good judgment will prevent us from heading south before we should."

"Did you fellows hear what Sam said?"

"Yes," said Andrew as he picked up more of the long strips of meat, "and I think Sam's right; it's time to get rid of the furs and then we'll know where to go from there."

"Sooner or later the Blackfeet will decide to pay us a visit," Sam told them, "and that's another good reason to change our location."

Excitement shone on all their faces. They were beginning to reach their goal and even though they would miss the life they were now living, they all thought they'd like ranching even more.

They packed their pelts and all supplies needed to begin somewhere else, and headed westward, toward Fort Hall. Sam scouted ahead, four or five hundred yards, and Carolyn followed. Arthur rode behind his sister, then came the pack train, and at the rear rode Andrew. All were seasoned hunters and trappers, ready at a moment's notice to attack or repulse an aggression by an enemy. Their eyes searched automatically for any conceivable sign of danger as the silent column moved slowly into higher country. Over the highest mountain and down the west side of the mountain range lay Fort Hall, on the Snake River.

Birds of many different species could be heard as they sang their own distinctive songs. Western blue birds, their colors flashing in the sunlight, flew ahead of them. A Steller's Jay sat on an overhead branch, scolding them as they passed beneath, and a redtailed hawk swung high in the sky in front of them.

Carolyn mused about what a different life they led out here, compared to New Hampshire life. She preferred, vastly, the life they had led here in the mountainous west, even with the need to be alert constantly, in order to survive. The feel of being and living so in touch with nature was so fine, so clean, so basic. She only wished her parents had survived to live out here. Surely they would have loved it as much as she and her brothers did.

Her eyes looked ahead every few seconds to watch Sam, to see if he made any sign to signify danger. A cool breeze blew in from behind them, from the east, and Carolyn adjusted her rifle and turned in her saddle to look back at her brothers and the pack train. As she turned back, she saw that Sam was sitting motionless and Buck resembled a statue, so still did he stand. Now the only movement which Carolyn could see as she motioned for her brothers to stop, was Buck's head as he turned it toward the southwest and pricked his ears. She sniffed the air and her brothers did also and they seemed to scent fresh blood. Sam had dismounted now, and signaled to the others to remain on their mounts.

Rifle at the ready, Sam crouched and moved silently into the underbrush. In a few minutes he reappeared and motioned to the others to approach. They dismounted and drew nearer, cautiously, until they could see what Sam was watching.

Sam pointed to a wolf who was eating on the hindquarters of an elk. The elk's eyes showed fear and hopelessness as it lay motionless and the wolf continued to chew on the haunch. Sam jumped forward toward the wolf, waving his arms to scare him away from the downed elk. However, the wolf just raised his head and stared at Sam as if to say, "Get your own meat."

Sam stooped and picked up a rock and Carolyn and her brothers were ready in case Sam needed help. The wolf looked at Sam and bared its teeth as if preparing for an attack. Sam threw the rock, striking the wolf on the side. It jumped back a few inches, seemed to be considering, and then after one more look at the four humans, decided it was best to retreat. The elk lay there for some time, then slowly heaved itself to its feet and staggered into the underbrush.

"Poor thing," Carolyn whispered, "will it live?"

"It might," Sam replied, "crippled animals such as elk, deer, and buffalo are often seen with scars over much of their bodies, showing where other animals have feasted on them." He raised his hand, asking, "Do you hear anything?"

"No," whispered Carolyn.

"Neither do I," Sam replied. And it was true that not a sound could be heard, a sure token of danger. Sam pointed in the direction of the horses and they all moved that way. They were where they'd left them, but Sam could still sense something amiss. He continued to sniff the air and the others followed his example.

"Indians . . . Sioux," muttered Sam. "Miniconjou . . . bring the horses together and you three keep your eyes and ears peeled while I scout. They should be friendly, but those who take too much for granted, don't always live long."

Carolyn took charge as Sam slipped silently away from them. She motioned for her brothers to bring the horses to where she waited. Andrew tied a long rope between two trees and Arthur tied the horses along it quickly, while Carolyn kept a lookout; then her brothers joined her.

Meanwhile, Sam was moving forward in a crouched position from tree to tree, bush to bush, as his eyes searched for signs, and he listened intently. He suddenly received the impression that the danger could be behind him, near the other three, and he swiftly, but silently made his way back to them, afraid that he'd been decoyed away from them. He was seen by Arthur first, and from his prone position he motioned to his sister and brother and then pointed to Sam. Andrew and Carolyn nodded and resumed watching the forest around them, listening for strange sounds.

In seconds, Sam was back with them, "Why didn't they attack? They were smart enough to divide us at the opportune time, but they didn't attack. Why not?"

"Maybe they are friendly," Andrew suggested in a low voice.

"Could be, but we can't know for sure. Where do you sense the danger lies, Carolyn?"

Carolyn's head turned slowly as she sniffed and finally she pointed to their right. "At about the two o'clock position, and it seems there are only two or three of them. That's strange," she added quickly, "why send only two or three? To turn our attention from the direction where the real danger is?"

"I think you're right," conceded Sam, "and maybe they're just as confused as we are." As he continued to watch the surrounding area he said, "These are Miniconjou . . . I'm certain of that, but if they're friendly why are they still concealed?"

"Maybe they're not sure who we are," Arthur murmured softly as he crawled up beside Sam. "Why don't we give a signal that we are their friends?"

"Good point," Sam told him. All were silent as they studied the still forest ahead of them. The smell of pine needles penetrated their nostrils as the cool breeze from the east whistled through the treetops. Now and then a small creature darted through the underbrush, sometimes it was a squirrel, sometimes a chipmunk. They seemed to glide over the dry, brown pine needles with little effort, now and then stopping to inspect the terrain around them.

Sam's eye caught Carolyn's as she beckoned to him. "Stay here, Arthur," he whispered as he touched Arthur's shoulder, "Carolyn wants me."

"Right," Arthur acknowleged.

"Why don't you put your red Son of Manitou hat on one of the overhead branches?" Carolyn suggested. "If they are friendly, they surely will recognize that hat and communicate with us."

"Excellent idea." Sam moved backward to the pack horses and in a few minutes he was back with the red hat which he placed on the end of a long stick and then hung on the highest limb he could reach without exposing his position. They waited and after a long while, a voice called, "Is that you, Son of Manitou?"

With a smile on her face, Carolyn was about to stand, when Sam pulled her back, "It may be a trick. Who speaks to us?" he yelled.

"Little Hawk," came the reply, as he walked from behind a tree some distance away.

Sam and the others jumped to their feet and gave the Indian welcoming waves which were accompanied by broad smiles.

"What are you doing so far from your regular stomping ground?" Sam asked the young brave.

"Looking for glory, scalps, and horses which will bring us adavancement in our tribe," he grinned. "Where is the Son of Manitou going?"

"Over the mountain to Fort Hall, to sell our pelts," Sam told him, and then maybe come back for some more trapping."

Little Hawk offered to accompany them to Fort Hall to help insure them a safer journey. The rest of his party, except for him and his two cousins, were a few miles back, but when they arrived, there would be twelve more of them to accompany Sam and his party. Little Hawk welcomed the opportunity to ride with Sam, for he believed, as did the rest of his people, that it was good luck to associate with lucky people, and they believed that Sam was special. Accordingly, he suggested further, "There are many beaver in my country; why don't you come and live in my village while you trap?"

"That just might be a good idea; we may take you up on it," Sam said heartily.

"It would be an honor," said Little Hawk, earnestly.

Fort Hall was located on the south side of the Snake River, and as Sam and his party approached the fort, Indians from many tribes could be seen going in and out of the fort. Tepees were pitched along the outer walls of the fort. Fur trappers of every size and description could be seen talking together or lounging against the walls.

Another pack train could be seen winding down a trail from the north, still at some distance from the fort. The pack train had several riders escorting it. While some trappers preferred to trap by themselves, others sometimes made up a party and worked together.

Sam led his outfit toward the fort, his rifle cradled in his arm. Carolyn rode directly behind with her brothers riding to either side of her and they also had their rifles ready. Behind them came the pack horses, and Little Hawk and his braves rode together at the rear. They were a colorful sight with their buckskins decorated with bright bead and quill work. Little Hawk's pony had a red hand painted on its chest, indicating that he had killed an enemy with his bare hands. His coal black hair was plaited in two braids and on his head, as was the case with most of the others, he wore a round, fur hat without any visor. An eagle's feather was attached to the back of his hat, and a round, colorful decoration had been sewn to the front of his hat.

The squaws had used imagination and originality when they decorated with the quills which had been dyed many different colors, and unique and beautiful designs had been done with the quills. Religious symbols could be seen on the clothing of the warriors, symbols which they believed would protect them in battle.

On their shields could be seen religious designs which they believed were sent to them in visions by the spirits. The owner of a shield with these designs could expect to be protected from harm.

The business of unloading, and dealing with the trader had been concluded when Luis murmured to Sam, ''You had better be on your guard.''

''How do you mean?'' Sam asked him.

''The three Damurs brothers have been watching you pretty close ever since they saw you approach the fort. They're noted for following trappers after they have sold their furs, and waylaying them a few days out of here. You've gotten a good price for your trappings and I'm sure they know that by now.''

''What do they look like?''

''As you leave here, you'll not be able to miss them for they're sitting on the bench right outside the door. Their names are Pierre, who is the oldest, then comes Kitou, and finally Paul, the youngest.

They hail from Canada and no doubt Canada was glad to be rid of them."

"Thanks for the tip," Sam said as he and Carolyn and her brothers turned to leave the post. He turned back to say they'd pick up their supplies around in back.

"It was nice doin' business with you," replied the trader.

As they stepped out on the porch, Sam glanced casually at the three men sitting on the bench against the side of the building. They wore greasy buckskins that showed their wear, and Sam thought he'd never seen a more unsavory bunch. Well, I'll know them if I ever see them again, he told himself grimly.

"Howdy," he greeted them.

"Howdy," Pierre replied. "I think this is going to be a good year for the trappin' don't you?"

"Guess it all depends on where you trap," was Sam's noncommittal reply.

"Yep, I guess you're right about that. Beaver are where you find them. Are you goin' out again?"

Sam's reply was, "Good day to you." He strode off the porch and walked toward Carolyn and the others who were already mounted. As he put his toe in the stirrup, he told them they'd pick up their supplies behind the trading post and as they rode toward the back, he told the others to take a good look at the men seated in front of the post.

"Hello, Little Hawk,' Kitou said, "I didn't know you'd taken to trappin' with that big mountain man."

"Kitou," was the only reply Little Hawk gave to the Frenchman as he nodded his head.

When they had loaded their supplies on the pack horses, they rode away from the fort, and after a few miles, Sam dropped back to question Little Hawk. "What do you know about the Damurs brothers, my friend?"

"That they are bad medicine," came Little Hawk's quiet reply.

"Would they be apt to attack a party as large as this?"

"No, but those three are not afraid of anything or anyone. I think we've not seen the last of them. Our opportunity for glory may come sooner than we expected," he grinned.

Little Hawk changed the subject, "Have you considered spending some time at my village? You know you and your family would be very welcome."

"We've talked it over and we'd like that," answered Sam. "But first I have a plan which may rid us of the Damurs if they come after us; that is, if you'd like to be a part of it.''

"You know that without asking," grinned Little Hawk, "tell it to me!''

"I'm sure you're aware that they're following us," continued Sam, "hoping to get hold of the money we received for our pelts. Now if they think we've split up, you going back toward your people, and our tracks leading in another direction, we can catch them off guard by having you circle back behind them. Then when the time is right, we'll strike at them.'' Sam elaborated a little more on the plan before he rode back to the front of the column.

CHAPTER X

T he three Damurs brothers rode out of Fort Hall not long after Sam's party had left. They were a ragged looking outfit, with their scruffy beards stained with tobacco juice and their long matted hair. All wore moccasin boots which extended to their knees, and two wore fur hats while Pierre was bareheaded.

Each carried a rifle cradled in an arm. Kitou had a leather strap around his neck from which hung his skinning knife in its sheath. Pierre and Paul had theirs attached to their belts. They all gave off an odor resulting from very few baths in the recent past.

"How much do you suppose they got for those pelts?" Pierre wondered aloud.

"Don't know, but I'd bet it's enough for us to be interested," Paul gloated.

"They looked like grade A pelts to me," interrupted Kitou, "and if they were, they got top dollar for them."

Kitou and Paul accepted their older brother, Pierre, as the leader of their little bandit unit, and as they rode along, he continued to look at the ground to either side of his horse.

"They weren't expecting us to follow them," he said as he leaned to study the trail, "so let's make sure it stays that way." He looked from one to the other of his brothers, "Do you understand, both of you? Well, say something!"

"Sure," they both answered almost simultaneously, "you're the boss."

"Look," Kitou pointed out, "they're splittin' up, the Indians are going north and the others continuin' east."

"Good," Pierre commented with satisfaction as he stood in his stirrups and looked down at the party in the valley far below. "They must be an hour's ride ahead of us, and darkness will come in about an hour, too. They'll be making camp soon. Let's get down off this hill before dark and then we'll wait until they're sound asleep before we strike!" He chuckled, "They'll never know what hit them!"

"How far back are they?" Sam asked as Arthur turned in his saddle to glance back up the hill.

"They're at the top of the hill, just starting down," Arthur told him.

"Don't see how they've managed to stay in business so long, they're so obvious," muttered Sam as he grinned at Arthur.

"Let's hope we're not just as obvious," answered Arthur.

The sun had gone behind the hill and it was growing dusk when they found a good camping site. A small stream tumbled down the rocky hillside and widened to a small pool before it continued on its way across the floor of the valley. There was shelter, water, and good grass for the horses along the stream.

"Plenty of good cover to confuse our friends when they come," Andrew said.

While Andrew and Arthur took care of the horses and made camp, Sam and Carolyn went in search of fresh game, bringing back a fat turkey they'd caught roosting in a tree. As they ate, Sam told them of his plan. "My guess is that they'll wait until they think we're asleep, for that kind doesn't take any unnecessary chances. So let's confuse them. We'll extend the appearance of our sleeping bags to perhaps twice the length they are ordinarily, using logs or whatever we can find, making it appear a clumsy effort to show them we're still sleeping by the fire. They'll believe we were just careless in attempting to fool them, that in reality we're back somewhere in the brush. But we'll really be in camp.

"They'll either look for us there and Little Hawk will get them, or they'll wait for another time to strike. If they don't fall for the plan, Little Hawk will still get them, but I'll bet my life they'll fall for it."

The Damurs watched from afar as Sam and the others prepared to turn in for the night. Scattered clouds obscured the moon from time to time and they couldn't see the camp while the moon was behind the clouds. Thus, when they drew nearer, quite a while later, Pierre chuckled to himself.

"What are you snickering about?" Kitou asked his brother.

"They must think we are stupid . . . look at those blankets . . . so much longer than they would be if they were really sleeping in camp. They're really sleeping somewhere back in the bushes. But that Sam fellow is no dummy, so we'll have to be careful. We can still sneak up on them and maybe we'd better knife them. Let's give them a couple more hours to get to sleep soundly."

"How did they know we were following them?" wondered Kitou. "I thought we'd kept at a safe distance, out of sight."

"They're mountain trappers," whispered Pierre, "they probably picked up our scent or sensed danger. Those people are good at such things. If they were not, they wouldn't be alive today, but this is one time we'll outsmart them."

Paul and Kitou smiled as they nodded, and Paul whispered confidently, "They'll have to be smarter than that to trick us!"

"They're close by," whispered Sam, "be ready just in case Little Hawk's braves miscalculate."

"Phew, what an odor!" Arthur muttered.

"Shhh," his sister cautioned.

It seemed much longer than it actually was before anything happened, then, instead of the rustling of the leaves caused by the evening breezes, and the sound of running water, there came the war cry of Little Hawk's braves, and at the sound, Sam, Carolyn, Andrew and Arthur threw back their blankets and rose almost as one, with their rifles in their hands, and rushed to offer aid if it was needed, but it was all over, and the braves had already taken scalps.

"I think we're ready now to go with you to your village," Sam told Little Hawk.

They rode up out of the valley the following morning just as the sun rose over the mountain ranges to the east. Little Hawk took the lead and the others followed in single file. Spring was far advanced and the forest was a soothing, peaceful blend of many soft colors, from the pale greens of the new leaves of the hardwoods to the dark greens of the pines and cedars, to the silvery bluegreens of the spruce. Shadows stretched their fingers over the landscape as the sun slowly moved across the blue sky. An occasional white fluff of cloud drifted northward. The bark of the trees added color to the scene, with tones ranging from the pale aspen and birch to the many darker shades of brown. This rainbow of colors was sometimes reflected from pockets of water which had collected from a recent rain or a bubbling spring which leaped and tumbled along its rocky course.

The riders seemed steeped in beauty, and Carolyn reflected that indeed they "walked in beauty" as Indian philosophy put it.

The line of riders moved slowly through the trees, across a small stream now and then, and over rough terrain, as it made its way toward the village of Little Hawk.

As they crossed a small mountain meadow, Sam caught up to ride beside Carolyn saying, "You know, because of the outdoor life we lead, in the sun and wind, we're as brown as the Miniconjous. Look at your skin color; it's a beautiful tan, and that is true of your brothers, also."

"Don't leave yourself out," Carolyn told him with a smile, "and besides, I love your freckles!"

A few days later, Andrew turned in his saddle to look back at Sam and remarked, "I can smell smoke."

"We must be near the village," Sam answered, as he rode on up the line of braves until he reached Little Hawk. "How much farther?"

"Three, maybe four miles," was his reply. They rode side by side in silence until they reached a small river. Little Hawk and the others splashed across and upon reaching the other side, turned to ride upstream on the dry, sandy bank. The smell of the camp smoke was growing stronger and before long the village came into view. Dogs barked and much activity could be seen in the village as Little Hawk led his party toward it. Tepees covered many acres along the river's edge, and many of them had smoke spiraling lazily from their smoke holes. A man with a brightly colored blanket wrapped around his shoulders stood near the closest tepee and his squaw tended a fire while two children helped her.

Grey Eagle came out of his lodge dressed in light colored buckskins which were beautifully designed and decorated. He welcomed his son and his braves with dignity, then smiling broadly, welcomed Sam and his party, "My people and I welcome a true friend and brave warrior and his friends!"

They dismounted and clasped his hand in firm handshakes. The chief threw back the flap of his tepee and motioned for his guests to enter his lodge, saying that someone would care for their horses. He motioned for them to be seated around the small fire in the center of the lodge.

Then, in a gesture of peace and friendship, he passed the peace pipe after he had taken four puffs and blown smoke in the four directions. He passed the pipe to Sam, holding it in both hands, in ceremonial fashion. Sam and each of the others then solemnly followed the example of the chief.

CHAPTER XI

T he women of the village gathered to build two tepees, one for Sam and Carolyn, the other for Andrew and Arthur.

Tall, straight young saplings had been selected, cut, peeled, and transported to the village. The six women who came then to erect the tepees were cheerful and playful as they approached the location where they would erect them. They seemed to be enjoying themselves, perhaps because they had a chance to visit, to get caught up on all of the latest news and gossip. It was obvious to the onlookers that they were experienced at what they were doing.

One woman held a stake to the gound while another unraveled a rawhide rope from a small stick about the thickness of a man's thumb and perhaps a foot long. She attached one end of the rope to the stake and then walking to the end of the rope, dragged the stick in a circle as she walked around the stake, making a perfectly round circle on the ground. With their digging tools, the women began removing the ground from within that circle to a depth of about six inches, then four women with sharpened buffalo bones to form blades, began to level the ground while the other two brought water from the river and sprinkled it on the excavated, flattened surface. All then packed the damp earth with their feet until it was smooth and hard.

Then they made a larger circle, using the same method as before, this one about three feet wider than the original circle. twenty-five tepee poles were then butted onto this line and tied at the top with rawhide ropes. Buffalo hides had been sewn together to cover these poles and a liner then sewn part way up on the inside of the tepee wall and folded inward so that it extended out over the unexcavated benchlike portion of the lodge. This would vent any draft from blowing onto the occupants as they slept on the bench. The women next gathered armfuls of grasses to place on the bench until they thought their guests would be comfortable sleeping. Robes were then spread on top of the grasses. And as a final touch, the women went to the woods and selected choice branches from the thick brush, cut them and tied them to make tripods on the benches at regular intervals and covered them with buffalo robes.

Arthur said to his sister, "Carolyn, I can't believe what I just saw. Those tripods covered with robes make perfect back rests. And the space behind the robes makes a perfect storage area!"

"They've had a long time to perfect their building methods, you know, Arthur," replied his sister, "and they're certainly skilled at it."

"And not a wasted motion, either," her brother enthused.

While the construction of the tepees was going on, Sam and Andrew decided to ride out and have a look for good trapping areas.

Meanwhile Carolyn had moved their things into the lodges and Arthur had killed an elk and had been extremely careful not to forget the Indian custom of giving the spirit of the departed animal the utmost respect and courtesy which his station deserved. Seeing this, the Indians were relieved and pleased that Arthur had not done anything to dishonor their lifelong religious traditions when he had killed. Arthur had made sure that the unwanted parts of the elk were placed high in a tree, so that the dogs couldn't reach them. He had earlier shown the highest respect for the elk when he spoke to the spirit of the dead animal, for the Indians believed that all animals have souls, that they are the spiritual equal of man. They believed that if an animal's soul was mistreated, it could communicate with the spirits of animals yet living, and these animals would leave the area where the desecration had occurred, thus leaving the Indians with no animals to hunt.

Sam had cautioned his family that sometimes the Indians mourned the death of an animal, especially that of a bear, as though it were the death of a relative. Some would go as far as openly crying for the dead animal. The bear was one of the most highly respected of the animals which the Indians hunted, and they often apologised to the bear and asked to be forgiven for having to kill it. It was thought by some of the medicine men that their own souls dwelt within the bears.

After Arthur had climbed down from the tree in which he had

placed the remains of the dead elk, he walked back to Carolyn's tepee and suggested, "Why don't we offer some of the elk meat to the others?"

"Not just some of it, Arthur. Have you forgotten what Sam told us?"

"What was that?"

"When some member of the tribe is fortunate enough to have had good luck in hunting, he always shares his good luck. We are members of this tribe now, so we must share the elk meat with the others. Ask Little Hawk to tell the people that we wish to share our good fortune."

Little Hawk was cooking a large trout over his fire when Arthur approached and he got to his feet and said, "Welcome to my dwelling."

"Thank you, Little Hawk," came Arthur's reply. "We want to invite the other members of the tribe to share in the elk which I killed, but Sam isn't here and Carolyn and I don't know how to do this in the proper way. Could you help us?"

"It would give me great honor to help you and the others will be extremely pleased that you wish to do this. This will show them, as nothing else could, that you are one with us, that you believe in and participate in our ways."

He turned back to the fire, adjusting the fish, making sure that the head of the fish was facing upward upon the roasting sticks.

"Why did you arrange it that way?" asked Arthur, curiously.

"Because," Little Hawk explained, "our customs teach us that fish also must be properly caught, cleaned, cooked, and eaten. If this is not done, his spirit will tell the other fish to leave the river where we camp. We show our respect in part by having the head of the fish face upward. Also we must never let a fish touch the ground when we catch it, but must always place it on a pallet of leaves or a pelt, never directly on the ground. This is taboo and when the fish has been eaten, the bones must be returned to the river. This will please the spirit of the fish, for it would be extremely unhappy if dogs or others animals should get its bones.

"My people were hoping and correctly so, that you would honor our customs and respect the remains of the elk which you killed. They noticed how you placed the parts of the elk which you couldn't use, high up in a tree. This pleased them and they feel you are one with us.

"Now, I must tell them that you wish to share your hunt. Later, after the sun falls behind the mountains, we will have singing and dancing by our medicine men to thank the spirits of the elk and the fish for permitting us to use them for our food. Then the bones of the fish will be thrown back into the water.''

Later that evening Sam and Andrew came back from their scouting expedition and reported to Carolyn and Arthur that Little Hawk had been right, for there seemed to be many beaver in the rivers in the nearby mountains.

Sam was also pleased about the way in which Arthur had killed, and disposed of the elk, saying that it showed consideration for the feelings of their hosts.

During the remainder of their stay with the Miniconjous, the four participated wholeheartedly in the life of the village, and found the Miniconjous to be exceedingly good hosts, always considerate of the comfort and wishes of their guests. Thus they enjoyed thoroughly their stay in the village through the summer months, and in the fall began to prepare to take up their trapping once more.

All that trapping season, they trapped in earnest, and by spring enough furs had been trapped and seasoned to give them the added revenue which they needed for their stake farther south.

Although they looked forward to their new life, still they were saddened to tell the Miniconjous farewell. They were good and true friends, always courteous and thoughtful, and as they rode away from the village beside the river, they waved goodbye repeatedly.

CHAPTER XII

They were headed for the cabin at the headwaters of the Green River, for they wanted to see it one last time before they traveled south to Fort Bridger.

"Well, it doesn't look too bad," Sam commented as he sat looking at their former home.

"We won't have much to do to it, if anything," Carolyn answered as she swung off her horse and walked toward it, "we're only going to stay here a few days, anyway."

"Carolyn," Sam called as he dismounted, "be careful, there may be a critter inside."

Carolyn looked through the door and said, "You can say that again, Sam. It looks as though a couple of grizzlies fought a war in there."

The rest joined her to look at the interior of the cabin and agreed that the outside appearance had certainly been deceiving, for the inside was a disaster.

"I don't know how the rest of you feel, but I don't think it's worth the trouble to clean it up," Andrew said, "why don't we make a camp outside and in the morning head for Fort Bridger?"

"I think Andrew is right," Arthur shook his head as he walked back to his horse, "why should we clean up that mess?"

"Well, let's prepare to camp then," Sam said as he also turned away from their old home. "Carolyn and I will scout the area a little and while we're at it, we'll rustle up some supper. Why don't you two take care of the horses and get a fire going?"

That evening they sat beside the fire talking about their

many adventures and their hopes for the future.

They had struck camp and were well on their way to Fort Bridger by daybreak. They looked back at the cabin for one last time and all agreed with the comment made by Carolyn, "A lot of good memories were made in that cabin and we'll not forget. Mother Nature furnished us with our future and we thank her for that."

"Hear, hear," the others added as they reined their horses in the direction of Fort Bridger.

Their first night out, they were due to receive a visit from the Blackfeet, who hoped to even the score with red hat, the Son of Manitou, the hated white man who had been responsible for the deaths of their young braves, for sending them to the world of the spirits. They had followed the four from a great distance, for their respect for the power of the tall mountain man to detect danger was immense.

Fifteen Blackfeet dismounted and hobbled their horses several miles from the Sidwell camp. Their scout had come back to report that their enemies were camped for the night, and to avoid detection, they went forward on foot with great caution, for they were taking no chances in getting their revenge.

Some time after the Blackfeet had hobbled their horses, two men caught the scent of horses, but not of men. Thor looked at Many Horses in One, or Lone Wolf, as he preferred to be called, and with a puzzled expression on his face asked, "What do you make of it?"

"Maybe wild horses?" came the query in return.

"Let's check it out," Thor said as he put his horse into a lope. They pulled in their horses on the edge of a long meadow and studied the fifteen hobbled horses who were grazing before them.

"Blackfeet," Thor said, looking at his companion.

"You're right, my friend, but what are they up to? We'd better find out."

The two men rode the high ground so they could observe the terrain below without fear of detection and before long they spotted a camp far below them, not far from the Green River.

"Now we understand what the Blackfeet are up to," Thor said as he leaned on his saddle horn and stared down at the camp.

"Do you see anything familiar about that camp, my friend?" Lone Wolf asked.

Thor turned to study the far away figures, then in a flash turned to his companion. "It's Sam; only he would wear that red hat!"

"Now look upstream," Lone Wolf pointed back up the river, "What do you see?"

"There's our Blackfeet," Thor acknowledged.

Sam was restless, "I feel something is wrong, feel it in my bones, and think it is upriver from us. What do you think?" He looked around at the others who were busily working around the camp.

"Let's go downstream a way and then circle back through the trees," said Andrew. "If it's upstream, at least we're downwind."

"Before we go, let's pad our bedding with rocks, wood, or any object which can pass for figures under blankets," suggested Sam, "then we'll build up the fire a little."

After this was done, they melted away into the willows which bordered the river and stole along the river bank for quite a way before they doubled back through the trees at some distance from the river. When they could see the campfire flickering through the leaves they crouched, watching for any sign of trouble. All waited in silence as Sam quietly climbed a tree and braced his back against the trunk so that he could watch their horses for any sign of disturbance. Suddenly, one of the horses threw up his head and pricked his ears forward, and Sam could see a bush move ever so slightly. The other horses also lifted their heads and gazed in that direction and now Sam could see the Blackfeet crouched, and crawling, inching forward toward the campfire. Sam signaled the others to look in that direction and be prepared for action.

The Blackfeet were spread out, covering an area of perhaps fifteen yards and were moving cautiously but steadily toward the camp. When they reached the perimeter of the camp, one raised his hand and pointed to the bedding and seemed to be assigning more than one brave to each bed.

Sam raised his rifle, took aim, and squeezed the trigger and saw a Blackfoot sink to the ground. This was the signal for the others to act and gunfire could be heard from several quarters as the Indians took cover. Five down and at least ten to go, Sam told himself.

When Arthur had fired his shot, there was a brave only a dozen feet from him and Arthur didn't see him as he crept up behind with his tomahawk raised to strike. A thud was heard as Arthur turned to see the Indian fall with a knife in his back. Wondering, Arthur glanced around with a puzzled air.

After her first shot, Carolyn saw a Blackfoot slip behind a tree. He'll come out from behind that tree in a moment, she told herself, and when he does, I'll bet he comes out the same way he went in. She gambled as she aimed her rifle at that side. In a few seconds, the Blackfoot's face appeared in her sights and she pulled the trigger. The Indian's face disappeared in a mass of blood, but before Carolyn could notice the Blackfoot who was poised to slit her throat, a bloodcurdling yell echoed through the forest as Thor blew the brave's head off at eight paces. Hearing that yell caused Sam to repeat it from a short distance away, and the remaining Blackfeet retreated in terror, at a run. Lone Wolf got one more as he ran in his direction, stepping out in his path with his bowie raised.

The element of surprise which the Blackfeet had hoped to employ to vanquish their enemies had been met with failure.

There was much shaking of hands and clapping of each other's backs when the chaos died down and the old friends greeted each other.

"Your timing hasn't lessened any over the years, old friend," Sam told Thor as he shook his hand.

"It's a right good thing you have these young people to protect you, you old son of a gun," joshed Thor.

He and Lone Wolf were impressed with the fine looking young people who were now Sam's family, and Carolyn and her brothers were glad to meet Thor and Lone Wolf at last.

"Funny, how things work out," commented Thor. "When you rode out of the village that day, you sure didn't expect to meet your future bride so soon. You're a lucky man, Sam; most of us don't have that kind of luck."

"If it hadn't been for Sam, I don't know what would have become of us," Carolyn countered, soberly.

"Well, it turned out fine for all of you, and that's what counts," Thor said heartily. Lone Wolf looked around the circle of faces, smiling quietly.

They sat around the fire relating their adventures since they had last met for a long time that night, and as Lone Wolf and Thor ate some of the food which Carolyn had warmed for them, Thor asked her where she'd learned to cook like that. "No wonder Sam latched on to you. You wouldn't want to sell her, would you, Sam?" he grinned.

"How many horses would you give for her?" Sam teased as he looked at Carolyn.

"Guess there aren't that many," Thor laughed, "not from the way you two gaze at each other!"

Carolyn and her brothers learned more that evening about the life which Sam had led while living with the Mandans, learned much which Sam's modesty had prevented him from relating. And before they turned in for the night, the Fredericks had told of their adventures, beginning with their departure from Derry, New Hampshire.

"If it were not for us Yankees," Carolyn joked, "Sam would still be wandering in these hills trying to find himself, and I doubt if he is smart enough to accomplish that task by himself."

"I found you, didn't I?" Sam interrupted her with a chuckle.

"It's good to hear laughter and joking," Thor told them, "may bad times never cross your paths."

"I'll have to agree with Thor on that, if on nothing else," spoke up Lone Wolf, grinning.

CHAPTER XIII

T he following morning, the two groups separated once more, Thor and Lone Wolf turning again to the high country and Sam and his party continuing on down the Green River toward Fort Bridger.

"Watch your hair!" Sam yelled in farewell to his two friends, as they rode out of camp.

"Watch your own!" the two mountain men yelled in reply as they waved goodbye.

"I wish they had come with us," Carolyn said to Sam as she put her toe into her stirrup and swung into the saddle. "Friends like them only come once in a lifetime."

"Life has many paths, my darling, and all of us sooner or later reach that fork in the road. I've taken this path and they've chosen another. That's life, and only time will tell whether our paths will cross again."

"Now you're a philosopher, honey," Carolyn said as she leaned across to squeeze his hand. "I like to hear you call me darling, too, do you know that's the first time you've called me that? It sounds nice." She squeezed his hand again before she turned to her brothers saying, "Ready, you guys?"

"Let's stop the mushy stuff and move out," Arthur replied, with a chuckle. "I hope I never get married and act like you two."

"The innocence of youth," Carolyn said as she looked at Sam and trilled, "We're ready, d-a-r-l-i-n-g!"

She wore that utterly captivating look on her face which Sam found so irresistible.

He countered with, "That's as close as you're ever going to get to a drawl, honey, with that New England accent of yours!"

Andrew rode by them with a mock frown on his face, "I hope all this nonsense won't rob you of your common sense. After all, we're still in enemy country, you'll remember."

"Yes, sir, Mr. Frederick," Carolyn responsed as she mocked her brother with a military salute.

As Andrew looked back at them, he wore a happy smile as he said, "Watch out world, the team of Sidwell and Frederick are on their way."

Fort Bridger was more like a series of log cabins that interlocked, rather than a fort. The logs were notched in the same fashion as the structure of a cabin except that the gate was constructed of vertical logs, and the fort was smaller than the Fredericks had expected.

"Any structure, whether it be a house or barn, that can serve as a fort in time of trouble is called a fort," Sam explained to the others. "Where we're headed, many houses are constructed of adobe or earth bricks, and some of those houses have walls which are two feet thick or thicker. Neither arrows nor bullets can penetrate such walls, so those structures could be classified as forts also, even though they serve as dwellings."

"Hello, the fort!" he yelled, as he finished his explanation.

"Welcome," a voice said, as the gates swung open. The gates were opened in the morning and remained open until nightfall unless there was a reason to do otherwise. They seemed to be the first arrivals that day.

Sam and his party rode through the gate and found Jim Bridger standing on his porch. "Welcome to Fort Bridger, stranger," Jim said as he eyed the pack animals. "It looks as if you've done pretty well for yourselves."

A few white men were coming out of the buildings now, one man pulling his suspenders over his homespun shirt as he stepped from one of the doors.

Three Indians had followed them into the enclosure, coming from the direction of some tepees which were ranged along the wall of the fort.

"Yes," replied Sam as he dismounted and shook the hand which Jim Bridger extended. "These are all first quality pelts, Mr.

Bridger."

"That's what they all say," replied Jim with a chuckle, "let's see what you have."

Sam, Andrew, and Arthur began to unload the pack animals while Carolyn stood by, watching. The bundles of pelts were taken into the fort and stacked on the crude counters.

"Mostly beaver," Sam told Jim.

Jim looked through them as he puffed on his pipe. Some of them he raised close to his face as he volunteered, "My eyes, they're failing me." While he inspected the pelts, he asked, "Where are you headin' from here?"

"South, to Santa Fe," Sam replied, as he watched Bridger.

The others were behind Sam. Andrew leaned against the door frame and glanced outside from time to time. Carolyn was to Sam's left, and her eyes explored the inside of the trading post, and Arthur just watched Jim Bridger closely, as the old fellow handled the pelts expertly. All of them had their rifles cradled in their arms.

"Top notch crew, you have with you, mister," Bridger said, without looking up from examining the furs.

"The name's Sam Sidwell, and this is my wife Carolyn, and her two brothers, Andrew, there by the door, and Arthur here," he rested his hand on Arthur's shoulder.

"Well, Sam," Bridger said, after he had inspected the furs, "they're good pelts, and I'll give you top price. Will you let me trade with you or do you want to take them on to Vegas or Taos?"

"We'll sell here," Sam told him, "you've a reputation for being a fair and honest man Mr. Bridger. We were told right."

"Who told you that?" inquired Jim, idly.

"Thor Elkinson and others," was Sam's reply.

"Thor!" Jim raised his voice as he smiled. "How is that rascal?"

"Fine — we left him just a few days back. We camped a night together — with him and Lone Wolf."

"That's Many Horses in One, the breed, isn't it?"

"That's right."

"I've heard tell about him and about you four. Quite impressive, too. Your wife must be the mountain woman I've heard tell about. Most that come here say they wouldn't want to get on the wrong side of her."

"Very wise men," was Sam's comment, as he smiled at his wife.

Jim looked at Carolyn and asked, "How did you become a

mountain woman of such skill? Your reputation is talked of by both the mountain men and the Indians who come by — I guess you're the only mountain woman in these parts, at least I haven't heard of any others."

"Sam," she smiled as she nodded in her husband's direction, "is a good teacher."

Sam took the gold which Jim paid him for the pelts, and placed it in a leather pouch. He shook hands with Jim Bridger again saying, "It was nice doing business with you, Mr. Bridger."

"Jim's the name," was the gruff reply.

"It was nice doing business with you, Jim," Sam rejoined, "we'd better be on our way as soon as we stock up on supplies."

When some of the horses were reloaded, this time with food and ammunition, they told Jim Bridger goodbye, even though he'd extended an invitation to spend the night.

They had heard what a wonderful storyteller he was, and it was with regret that they didn't accept his invitation.

As they each shook Jim's hand, Sam told him, "It's been nice meeting you, for I heard about you back in Tennessee when I was small. It is an honor and a pleasure to meet up with you."

"The pleasure was all mine," Jim replied, "watch your topknots as you go south; those Apache and Comanche play for keeps."

Sam and Carolyn rode out through the gate of the fort side by side, with Andrew and Arthur riding together behind the pack horses. Later, as the trail widened out, the two young men rode up beside Sam and Carolyn and Arthur asked, "Do the Mandans have the same customs as the Miniconjous, Sam?"

"Yes, for they are part of the Sioux nation also, Arthur," replied Sam, "although there are probably slight differences between each tribe."

"We found out while living with the Miniconjous that they love celebrations to show their appreciation," pointed out Arthur.

"Most tribes have many ceremonies for various things," said Sam, "the Mandan, and the rest of the Sioux nation have their most important celebrations in the spring. One of them is to show respect and honor to the spirits who lower the water after the spring floods. Another, to celebrate the renewal of all life, from the birth of their children down to the new life of all animals, and they even give thanks for the new grass which begins to grow again in the spring. They do everything by fours — the ceremonies always take four days, with the most important part reserved for the fourth day. The reason for the importance of four is to give proper respect to the spirits of the north, south, east, and west."

"Is that why they blow smoke to the four directions when the peace pipe is smoked?" asked Arthur.

"Yes," Sam told him, and then continued, "when the young braves, around your age, Arthur, are initiated into the tribe as full members, the rites take four days, with the fourth day reserved for the best known, sometimes called the torture dance, but part of the Sun Dance ritual. In this dance, wooden skewers are fastened to sinews by ropes which were tied to the Sun Dance pole, the sacred pole around which the dancers whirl and strain until the skewers tear out of their flesh and release the young brave. They don't regard it as a form of torture, however, but merely as one more form of renewal, a part of life continuing."

Sam paused and glanced around at his listeners, "Have you had enough for now?" he grinned.

"I for one, find it fascinating," Carolyn told him, "how about you two?" She looked from one to the other of her brothers.

"I was just going to ask Sam which tribe he considers to be the most dangerous to the white man," said Andrew.

"Well, the Crows and the Blackfeet hate all white men and deal with them with any weapon which comes to hand, whether it be lying, treachery, or whatever it takes to kill white men. And we'll probaby find just as determined enemies in the Southwest. After all, we're encroaching upon what they consider their hunting preserves, and gradually ruining them, crowding them out little by little, so their attitude is certainly understandable, wouldn't you say?"

"We'd feel the same way if we were being pushed out," conceded Andrew, "and I don't know what the answer is, do you, Sam?"

"All I know for sure, Andrew, is that as more and more settlers come west, the Indian's problems with the white man, and our problems with the Indian will increase until solutions are found, and I hope those solutions will be fair to each of us."

"Well, our association with the Miniconjous taught us to think of their side of the problem," said Carolyn, "something not many white people will consider."

"Maybe there will be enough of us, when the time comes, to give them a fair shake, and at the same time consider the white settler's rights," Sam pointed out, "and with the more civilized tribes, it shouldn't be too hard to deal, but with tribes who have practiced human sacrifice, such as the Pawnee, we may have an uphill pull.

"The Pawnee would sacrifice a young maiden of the tribe to ensure that their fields would be fertile. Their sacrifice was made to placate the god of growth. Whether or not they still do this, I don't know."

"What do you know about the Indians in the Southwest, Sam?" Arthur asked, "Do you think they'll be as fierce as the Blackfeet, for instance?"

"I've heard that the Apache and Comanche are two of the most feared in the entire country, Arthur, and that some of their fiercest warriors are women. How many women join their war parties, I don't know, but some of them do, apparently."

"Sometimes it's necessary," said Carolyn soberly, "but I think it probably takes more toll on a woman than a man."

"There are men, also, who aren't able to assume the duties of a warrior in some tribes," said Sam, "and those men are forced to dress as women and otherwise take a woman's role, even to a name. From what I've heard this is their permanent station in life."

"Do you know what New Mexico Territory is like, Sam?" Andrew asked.

"That, we'll all learn together," Sam replied, "but I've heard of its beauty, mild climate, and fine grazing land."

CHAPTER XIV

About the middle of May, the four rode into Taos. Snow covered the ground as they rode down the narrow main street toward a trading post. For many years in its early history, Taos had been the scene of great fairs where the Spanish, Indians, and even French upon occasion, gathered to exchange goods. That time was gone, and the quiet of the village belied its rambunctious past.

They halted in front of the post, tied their horses to the hitching rack, and Sam, Carolyn, and Arthur went inside. Andrew leaned against one of the poles which supported the porch roof and cradled his rifle in his arm. His gaze roamed over the street, studying the people, buildings, and the surrounding mountains.

"Buenas dias," (good day) a man greeted him, as he strode past. Andrew nodded and smiled in return. People of all description, dress, language, and race passed him while he waited for his family to come out of the store.

New Mexico should be an interesting place to live, he thought to himself, as he watched two mountain men in buckskins ride by. They were followed by their pack string and an Indian who rode with them. They gave Andrew and his outfit a long look as they passed, but made no sign of recognition.

Two Mexicans were walking in the opposite direction, one with a serape slung over a shoulder. He said to the other one, "Cuan do venga Juan se lo dire."

Whatever he was talking about, I recognized the word, Juan, anyway, Andrew thought. Spanish is a pretty language and we're going to have to learn it.

"Well, we're ready," Sam said, as they came out of the store and crossed the wide, planked porch. "A couple of men in there told us that there's supposed to be good grazing land available south of here and west of the Pecos River. Said the grass is up to your horse's belly north of the mountain they call La Sierra."

"North?" queried Andrew, "I thought most mountains ran north and south."

"Well, this one has a mind of its own," grinned Arthur, "and it runs east and west. Sure sounds like good country down there!"

As they packed supplies on the horses Carolyn elaborated, "The government has a fort not too far from La Sierra, called Fort Stanton. The Indians, the Apaches, inhabit the White Mountains or Sierra Blanca as they call it, and that whole area is their stomping ground. Which is why grazing land is to be had for the taking, a lot of settlers aren't anxious to argue with them over land."

Sam tightened his cinch and mounted, "Let's ride on out a way and then we'll have a look at the map he gave us."

As they followed an old trail south, Sam told them, "The fellow in the store who told us about the area was through there not over a month ago. He says there is a beautiful little valley in the foothills south of the mountain and there are small Spanish settlements scattered along that valley. Placitas, which is the name of one of them, would be a good place to head to find out more about the whole area. What do you say we look into it?"

"I say we have a look at it," said Arthur, enthusiastically, "sounds like fine country and good grassland, just what we've been wanting. If we can make it in Blackfoot country, why not in Apache country?"

The others smiled at his enthusiasm, and Sam looked from Carolyn to Andrew, "Well, what do you two think?"

"Arthur's right," Carolyn said, as Andrew nodded his agreement. "I like this country so far," Andrew added, "let's give it a try."

The trail they were following entered a grove of giant old cottonwoods and it was here they decided to stop to study the map, to determine the best route to the southern part of the territory.

"What do you think, Sam? Don't you think you ought to decide, since you've had more experience at it than we've had?" Carolyn looked at her husband.

"All right," Sam traced with his finger across the map slowly. "We'll cross the Sangre de Cristo range here and follow the eastern side of the mountains until we reach Las Vegas. From there we'll follow the Gallinas River until we reach the Pecos River and then follow the Pecos until we reach the junction of the Pecos and the Hondo Rivers.

"The fellow back at the trading post said that'll give us a good idea of the country in the eastern part of the territory. We could follow the Rio Grande right down the line until we turned off east to reach the same location, but we wouldn't know as much about the eastern section."

Sam again traced the map with his finger saying, "Now at the junction of the Pecos and Hondo rivers, we turn west and start climbing up into the hills, but it shouldn't be rough going compared to some of the country we've been through. There are three rivers here." He bent over the map, studying it closely, "One of them, the Ruidoso goes up the south fork of one valley toward Sierra Blanca, while the Rio Bonito runs through another valley which will take us to Placitas, which is not far from La Sierra, as some people call it. The fellow at the trading post said the Indians call it 'The Mountains that Stand Alone'. Looks like the Hondo River is made up of the other two which meet at the junction. Well, how does that strike you?"

"Rio Bonito!" Carolyn mused, "What a pretty name for a river; I wonder what it means?"

Sam laughed as he gave her a hug, "That's exactly what it means, my dear, pretty, 'pretty river'."

They had ridden quite a few more miles when Sam suggested to Andrew that he scout ahead of them in search of fresh meat. This Andrew did and was lucky enough to spot a wild turkey roosting in a tree. He was plucking it when they rode into the campsite he'd selected.

As they ate their supper that night, Sam told them that the store keeper had said they could expect a milder climate in the south. Something they'd all been hoping to find.

"Stands to reason, after all, for it's been getting a little warmer even this much south," remarked Andrew. "It's bound to be more mild in the southern part of the territory." He continued, with a grin for his brother and sister, "After New Hampshire, we won't know how to act without wading in snow up to our stirrups!"

"Well, Tennessee had her moments, too," drawled Sam, "it usually didn't last very long, but we had pretty good storms at times, and we've seen our share of snow since we've been together. It won't be hard to get used to what they call an 'open winter' down there."

They had followed the Gallinas River for awhile a few days later when they suddenly saw ahead of them the Pecos, shimmering in the sunlight as it wound between its high, wide banks. "Now it feels like we're getting somewhere," Arthur said enthusiastically, "now all we have to do is follow it to where the Hondo River empties into it, and then ride up the Hondo."

"If we don't have any trouble, it shouldn't take us more than a week, or maybe less, to reach Placitas," Sam told them.

"One of the men we spoke to in Taos, said that the high plains are called the Staked Plains," Carolyn said, "do you know why, Sam?"

The four were riding through tall grass up to their horses' bellies, in many places. So far they hadn't seen any buffalo in the numbers they had been led to expect, but expected to do so at any time.

"Thor told me that a Spaniard named it that, or Llano Estacado, in Spanish, because he had to pound stakes into the ground at intervals as he explored eastward, in order to find his way back again. The plain resembles an ocean as the grass blows in the wind, and is probably just as hard to navigate without help," Sam told them.

"Is this part of the Llano Estacado, Sam?" asked Arthur

"Our map designates it as being east of the Pecos, Arthur, so I guess that's where they begin, right across the river there," replied Sam, "and they run for a long way eastward."

That night as they leaned back into their saddles near the fire, talking, Carolyn smelled him first, and froze, then looked upwind, and the others picked up the scent at almost the same time.

"A white man," said Carolyn softly, as she and the others reached for their rifles nearby.

"Over there in that clump of salt cedar," said Sam, moving away to investigate.

"Hello, the camp!" came the old man's yell.

"Come on in," responded Sam, not relaxing his vigilance.

The old timer was walking, leading two burros. He wore a grey beard which concealed most of his face, and his long grey hair reached his shoulders. An old, crumpled hat covered the upper part of his face, and he shoved it back on his head as he drew nearer to the fire. He carried a knife and a pistol at his waist, and in his right hand, he carried a long rifle. "That coffee sure smells good," he hinted with a grin.

Carolyn poured a cup and handed it to him.

"Thankee, Missy," he said as he squatted before the fire and drank from the cup.

He glanced at Andrew who was sniffing in the direction from which the old timer had appeared, and chuckled, "I'm all alone, sonny . . . you're mountain people, ain't ya? Most people ain't like you . . . don't notice much. It pays to be like you, though, you're livin' proof of that," he cackled.

"Do you live around here?" Andrew asked.

"I live everywhere, boy, go where I want . . . here and there . . . can't stay anywhere for long, and my partners go with me," motioning to the two burros who stood with lowered heads just at the edge of the firelight.

"Well, stay for breakfast, old timer," Sam invited as he leaned to pick up the coffee pot. "How about a little more coffee?"

"Don't mind if I do . . . don't mind if I do, young fella." When he had hobbled his burros, he came back to the fire, eager to talk to someone besides his partners. "Where you headed?" he asked as he sat down on his blankets.

"South," replied Sam.

"Good country, good country," the old man said as he stared into the fire, "good cattle country if the Apaches don't take your life."

The following morning the old fellow ate a hearty breakfast with the Sidwells and the Fredericks before he headed west, and they continued along the Pecos toward the southern part of the territory. They had asked him about the country around Placitas and he had grinned as he asked, "Do you know the whole name for Placitas? It's La Placitas Del Rio Bonito, means little places along the pretty river. Nice name and good people live there, farming people, hard working, but they know how to have a good time, too. Know how to give a dance or baile, as they call it. Live mostly in small settlements for protection from the Apaches. Good country over there. You ought to like it." He waved a hand, and talking to his burros, he started off briskly.

As they rode southward, Sam said, "Sounds like we're going to like the territory. Most of the settlers around Placitas are Spanish speaking so that means we'd better learn to speak Spanish also."

"That's what I was thinking," spoke up Andrew, "most people will usually treat you as well as you treat them, and that's what we should do with these new Americans, these Spanish

Americans. I'm going to learn their language, and I'm sure they'll learn ours and the same goes for the Apaches and the Comanches, if they'll give us the chance.''

"That's a good attitude to have, Andrew," Sam told him, "now if we can convey that attitude to our new neighbors, we should have no problem in getting along with them.''

Just then Carolyn reined in her horse and sat watching and pointing, "Look, Sam, wolves, I never saw so many together in one place!''

They had all stopped their horses and sat watching the wolves who glided in a grey mass across the horizon.

"It's my guess there's buffalo not too far away," Sam remarked.

"Do they follow the herds?" asked Arthur, glancing at Sam.

Sam was standing in his stirrups, looking in all directions. "Do you see any sign of coyotes?" he asked. "Wolves follow the buffalo, and a pack can bring down a cow or her calf, or even a crippled bull. Sometimes a bull will get crippled fighting another bull, and then the wolves finish him off. The coyotes clean up whatever the wolves leave.''

"I think I can smell the wolves," Carolyn said, "but I can't smell coyotes . . . but I can smell humans!''

"She's right, Sam," Andrew spoke up excitedly, "I can smell them too, and it's a strong odor. They're not trying to hide it, that's sure.''

"Probably buffalo hunters," Sam told them, "there must be a herd of buffalo somewhere near, so it follows that there are hunters after them, from what the old man said.''

As they reached the knoll of a small hill, Carolyn said, "Look, there's the herd, and it must be ten miles away at least. It extends all the way to the horizon, it's so large. My gosh, Sam, how could we raise cattle with those things around? They could carry our herds with them if they passed very near.''

"They don't usually graze too close to the mountains, from what I've heard," Sam told her.

Just then they heard a faint shot, and another, and then almost continuous shooting.

"The hunters have themselves a stand," Sam said, "they keep downwind of the herd, and I doubt if we can spot them, but look to the south and see if you can see anything moving. The skinners must be beyond those hills over there with their wagons, ready to move in and start their skinning.''

They all searched with their keen eyes in the direction Sam

had pointed, but no sign of either the hunters or the skinners was to be seen, although the sound of shooting continued.

"Why doesn't the herd run away?" Arthur asked.

"I've heard that buffalo can't see very far and as long as they can't see anything, the sight of one of them dropping doesn't seem to stampede them. The way the Indians buffalo hunt is something else, for they run right with the herd. The buffalo guns which these hunters use are said to weigh as much as a crowbar," he went on, "and they usually aim for the lungs or backbone, which drops him."

"We'd better go on," suggested Carolyn, and they continued on their way while still watching the far off herd.

A few hours later, as they rode at a brisk trot, Sam said, "Look to the east of us," he pointed at a large cloud of dust. "Stampede!" he told them. "Let's stop our horses and listen. If we can't hear them, we should be able to feel the ground shaking a little if we get off our horses."

"With that many buffalo stampeding, we might even feel the ground shake while mounted!" laughed Carolyn.

Sam had reined in his horse and sat listening and Andrew and Arthur had also, as Carolyn spoke, and she stopped also and listened. They could once more sense danger, and sat motionless, trying to assess the problem. Finally, Sam said softly, "Indians, but I don't know the odor, must be Apaches. We're in their country now. Let's move into the salt cedar along the river bank."

Nightfall came and went, and the four kept their vigilance. At sunup, the Apaches could be seen cautiously walking their horses toward where the buffalo had been slaughtered. When they had disappeared over the rolling ocean of a plain, the four turned their horses southward once more.

It was about noon one day when they pulled their horses to a stop on the banks of the Hondo and let them drink. The water was muddy.

"It must be raining up in the mountains," Sam said as he rested his hands on his saddle horn and gazed about them. They had ridden away from the Pecos and its thick stand of cottonwoods and salt cedars and had followed the Hondo toward the west. As they rode, the country took on a rolling appearance and they climbed gradually. The soil, though rocky, was covered with thick, curly grass which they would learn was gramma grass, one of the most nutritious of all for livestock.

In the distance directly ahead of them, they could see a

mountain peak, snow covered, and off to the northwest a lone mountain rose, it seemed up out of the plains. But as they progressed westward, they realized that they'd been looking at the eastern end of the mountain and that in reality it comprised a long range running east and west and they knew it was the one they'd heard about, La Sierra, where they hoped to settle, and their gaze often returned to look at it as they rode ever higher into the foothills.

When they had ridden for perhaps twenty or twenty-five miles up the Hondo, they made camp, and the next morning were well on their way by sunup. The air was crisp and cool and the warmth of the sun was welcomed by the four riders. They were pushing eagerly toward their destination and their interest in the entire landscape was intensified by the knowledge that they would probably be making their future home in this area.

A few hours later, after they had ridden through larger and larger foothills, they reached a high knoll and there below them, could be seen the twisting Hondo River as it carved its way through a beautiful, lush valley. Old walnut, box elder, and cottonwood trees lined the river as it rambled on its way toward the Pecos.

They followed a winding trail down off the hill toward the valley and finally reached the valley floor where they followed a road which closely paralleled the river. As they rode up the valley, they marveled at the quiet beauty surrounding them. A cluster of small adobe houses could be seen across the river and each house seemed to have its orchard, with fruit trees in bloom. Irrigation ditches sparkled in the sunlight as they carried the precious water to the gardens, fields and orchards.

They traveled onward, following the winding river, until Sam suggested they watch for a good camp site.

"There, by the river, under those large box elders would be a good place," suggested Carolyn.

Andrew touched Sam's arm just then and pointed. Up the river and on the north side, perhaps twenty-five deer were moving slowly toward the hills which rose out of the river valley.

"What do you think, Sam, shall we get a deer?" he asked.

The others sat their horses watching Andrew as he crept through the tall grass which was interspersed with juniper and cedar trees. He finally drew near enough for a good, clean shot, knelt on one knee, fired, and dropped one of the young bucks. The rest of the deer scattered, looking like kangaroos as they seemed to hop up the hillside.

As they sat before their fire that night, eating venison steaks, they talked about settling along the Hondo River, providing the valley stayed as wide as it was at that point. Pros and cons were discussed, but they finally decided to stay with their original plan. This valley was already getting settled, and they hoped to find more land, good for grazing, on the other side of the mountain.

Up early the next morning, they ate a hasty breakfast, and were on the way again, eager to reach their destination by nightfall. It was farther than they envisioned, however, and it would be the next day before they finally reached it.

As they continued along the river valley, they could see that in time of flooding, the peaceful little river could go on the rampage, reaching the wide river banks upon occasion. They had glimpsed the snow-covered peaks of Sierra Blanca from time to time and surmised that the snow runoff could bring the river up considerably before long. They didn't yet realize that flash floods occurred more often than spring flooding, and where the valley was the narrowest, it could sustain considerable damage. Hundreds of arroyos, some short and narrow, and others which could properly be called *canons*, extended for miles up into the higher country and could be truly awe inspiring when they ran during flash flooding. When these *canons* and arroyos emptied their rain water into the Hondo, that little river had many times overflowed its tidy banks, reaching its original banks.

As they rode further west, they found the valley became deeper and varied in width. The mouths of some of the rock-covered arroyos were one or two hundred feet wide at the point where they met the Hondo, while the river was probably an average of thirty feet wide at its low stage. Thus, it was easy to surmise how flooding could affect the river. Huge boulders which studded the banks of the river and the river itself, indicated something of the force and amount of water which came down periodically.

As they paused at the fork of the Hondo River, Sam commented, as he pointed to the right fork, "This must be where the Rio Bonito meets the Hondo and the left fork where the Ruidoso joins, as the map shows. The two, together, make up the Hondo. And according to the map, La Placitas is about ten miles up this valley."

Carolyn smiled, "I'm so anxious to see where we'll be living that it seems as though it's taken longer to ride from Taos than it actually has."

About three or four miles up this valley, which was narrower than the Hondo Valley, they noticed off to the left, on the south side of the Bonito, a little settlement perched on a bluff which overlooked the river. They learned from a small boy who was dangling a line into a quiet pool, that the little settlement was called Las Chozas, which meant houses in Spanish.

Fifteen or twenty of the little adobe and log plastered dwellings were scattered over the tableland. The little settlement looked peaceful in the sunshine. As they splashed across the Bonito and followed a little road which led near the settlement, they noticed that the people did extensive farming on the tableland. Fruit trees bloomed in a white and pink froth, and the giant old trees growing along the river contributed to the beauty of the area. The little wagon road hugged the river bank between the small settlement and the river, and within minutes, people appeared in their doorways, calling in Spanish to each other and to the newcomers, and waving.

Sam spoke to them in English, but they shrugged their shoulders, raised their hands, saying, "No habla ingles."

A small boy dashed importantly up the dusty street and was back almost immediately with a man who could speak broken English. He tipped his hat to Carolyn courteously saying, "Buenas tardes, senorita, senors, can we be of help to you? Will you get down?"

Carolyn smiled as Sam answered for them all, "We're headed for La Placita and then across the mountain."

The man looked at their buckskin clothing and their weapons, and laden pack animals and knew that they'd come a long way.

"Si, La Placita," he pointed up the valley, "about eight miles."

"Thank you senor," Sam told him as he tipped his hat to the ladies and reined his horse back to the little road. Carolyn and her brothers waved goodbye as they followed Sam.

"De nada," the man replied with a smile and a nod.

"We're going to have to learn to speak Spanish pronto if we're going to settle in these parts," commented Arthur as they rode away.

"Well now, younger brother," teased Andrew, "you're already speaking Spanish, throwing such words around so casually."

"Well, I've made a start then, big brother, gracias!"

Several miles further along, they came to a curve in the road and before them the valley widened out and in the distance they could see a little village. The hills were taking on a blue haze as the sun sank lower and the fresh green of the trees beside the river made the view a lovely one.

As they approached the little village, they noticed that most of the houses lay on the south side of the river, on higher ground. Across the river they could see cultivated fields and a pasture where horses and cattle grazed. As they neared the center of the town, they saw an adobe and stone tower three stories in height, around which a number of little houses were clustered. They later found these little houses were called jacals, and were built of upright poles, plastered over with adobe mud and roofed with sod.

The towers or torreons were to be found at intervals in the valley and were used as forts in times of attack by Apaches. This one presented a formidable appearance with its heavy walls and loop holes for defense.

"I wonder how many times they've had to take to the tower to escape the Indians?" speculated Andrew.

"There have been times when we'd have liked to have something similar!" laughed Sam. "Didn't they have a tower back at the other village?"

The long, winding street of Placitas was bordered on both sides by houses, cantinas, stores, and livery stables. With the exception of the rock walls which surrounded the patios, almost everything seemed to be built of adobe bricks, some of them plastered, some not.

They pulled up at a cantina and Sam dismounted, handing his reins to Arthur, telling them he wouldn't be long. He wanted to obtain as much information as possible before they continued on their way.

As he entered the dark interior, it took him a minute to get his bearings after the glow of the late afternoon light. He heard a question in Spanish from one side of the room, and walked toward the voice, beginning to use sign language, when a voice from a corner spoke, "He asked if he could help you."

Sam turned to see a man sitting behind a crude, homemade table.

"Would you tell him I'd like a beer?" asked Sam, thanking him.

"Uno cerveza, por favor, Filipe," the man told the bartender.

"Would you care to join me?" he asked Sam, as he rose to his feet.

"Thanks, I will," Sam replied, as he sat down at the stranger's table.

"The name is Pelletier, Paul Pelletier, and I'm from Canada, and don't ask what I'm doing so far from home," Paul said with a grin.

"My name's Sam Sidwell," Sam offered as he shook Paul's hand.

"I'm a has-been trapper," Paul went on as the bartender placed the beer in front of Sam, "and I'm roaming, looking for a place to settle these weary bones. From your dress, it looks as if you've been a trapper, too?"

"That's right and I have my wife and her two brothers outside waiting for me, so I won't stay but a minute. Maybe you can help me, Paul."

"Be glad to if I can; start asking."

It had taken longer than Sam had expected, and it was half an hour before he returned to Carolyn and her brothers. Paul Pelletier followed him outside and Sam introduced him to his family.

Carolyn asked Paul what part of Canada he hailed from, and he replied from Quebec.

"Why, we were acquainted with many people who settled in Derry, New Hampshire after moving from Quebec!" she exclaimed. "There are Pelletiers in Derry, perhaps related to you?"

"Pelletier is a common name in Canada, so it's not likely, although possible," Paul replied.

"Thanks Paul, your information has been a big help, and I hope we'll be seeing you again," Sam told him.

"He said there's a store where we can get supplies, and while we have the chance, we'd better do it."

"We've beat you to it, old boy," Carolyn said with a toss of her head. "Andrew and I left Arthur here while we stocked up, and still made it back before you finished. Thought there was no use in wasting time with two stops. Why don't we get a few miles out before we camp for the night?"

"The way I understand it," Sam said, "is that our best bet and straightest shot is up a canon a few miles west of here, called Salazar Canon. So why don't we make it to where we turn off and then camp?"

"Just as long as we camp early enough to give us time to get a good supper. Have a surprise for you and Arthur!" Carolyn promised, with a grin at Andrew.

Half an hour later, they had found a good campsite near the river, and while Sam and Arthur tended to the horses, Andrew stacked the packs to one side and helped his sister prepare supper.

They had bought salt pork at the little store, and Andrew fried it while Carolyn made biscuits and placed them in the dutch oven, covered it with hot coals, and then made coffee.

"When was the last time we had eggs?" she wondered aloud to Andrew. "Wait till Sam and Arthur see this!"

When the salt pork was well browned, Andrew began to break eggs in the iron skillet and after they were evenly done, he tenderly placed them on a tin plate, covered them, and began to make gravy from the drippings. "A meal fit for three kings and a queen," he muttered happily, as he worked. The biscuits, browned to a turn, came out of the oven, and the four gathered around to help themselves.

Sam and Arthur were complimentary enough to gratify Carolyn and Andrew immensely, and when Carolyn brought out the pot of honey, which they had bought at the little store, their happiness was complete. They hadn't had anything sweet for as long as they could remember, or at least since they'd left the village of the Miniconjou. So they really cleaned up on the biscuits and honey and drank their coffee with great satisfaction.

"Think this augurs well for our future," commented Sam, "somehow this country feels right to me; how does it feel to the rest of you?"

"I've a feeling we've found our home," Carolyn said as she leaned over to ruffle his hair, which gleamed in the firelight. Sam responded by hugging her to him, smiling down at her. Andrew and Arthur grinned at them both, pleased that they were so happy.

"This fellow, Pelletier told me a little about the area we're interested in, and the best way to reach it. From Salazar Canon, we cross over to what they call the Base Road and follow that until we reach the pass which is a canon running across the mountain. Using that, we ride through to the grasslands on the northern side of the mountain. Paul says it's fine rangeland, and there are two ranches located over there already. One is owned by Juan de Vargas who ranches to the west, and the other is quite a bit to the east and that rancher's name is Fernando Sisneros. He runs mostly sheep, but a few cattle up on this end of his place. In between the two ranches is a good sized piece of land still unclaimed, if we want it. They've both reached out and claimed the land they want."

"How much land could we claim?" asked Carolyn.

"It's about twenty or thirty miles between the two ranches, and nothing north of it for fifty miles or more," Sam told her.

"Boy, that would sure make us a great spread! Let's check it out before someone else has the same idea," piped up Arthur.

"Amen to that," said Andrew fervently.

They were up and on their way early the following morning, climbing steadily toward the Base Road, then paralleling the mountain for some miles till they reached the wagon road through the pass or gap, as it was called. That led them up through the tall, Ponderosa pine trees, some of them gigantic in size, with lichen growing on old trunks.

As they paused occasionally to breathe their horses and check the packs, they could see a long way down the trail behind them to the hills which bordered with the Bonito River. They were blue and shadowy in the early morning light, but later in the morning would assume a tawny appearance, stark in the clear morning air.

As they topped out and could see the grasslands lying before them, Carolyn gasped with delight, "Oh, what a beautiful sight."

"It is a wonderful rangeland," Sam commented, with awe.

For miles, they could see an ocean of prairie grass, with trees, streams, and enough rough country to furnish ample shelter for stock. From where they sat, it was hard to estimate how far they could see, for the land was a gently rolling terrain. Far off in the distance, farther than they could see, lay the Llano Estacado, the Staked Plains, where the buffalo ranged, that vast plain which they had paralleled as they followed the Pecos River.

They began their descent, exclaiming as they rode through the tall pines which gradually gave way to the shorter pinon, cedar and juniper trees which dotted the lower slopes of the mountain. As they reached the more level slopes, they turned eastward, riding slightly away from the mountain as they gazed on all sides, keeping watch for a place for their headquarters and ranch house which they hoped to build one day. They had ridden for perhaps an hour when they heard the sound of a rushing stream cascading down the side of the mountain. As they drew closer to the sound, they rounded a curve of the mountain and came to a lovely meadow through which the stream flowed, more sedately now that it was flowing over more level ground.

"Our homesite," Carolyn said softly to Sam.

"We could build our headquarters building and corrals down there, to the east of the meadow," her husband said excitedly.

"And our house right around here," put in Carolyn. "It's a lovely spot!"

"I don't want to be a damp blanket," warned Andrew, "but we'd better watch to see how much sunlight you'll get this close to the mountain. We'll want plenty of sunlight, but the mountain will shelter us if we don't build too far away from it," he conceded.

"What do you say we ride over our place a little more," Sam suggested, grinning, as he placed his hand over Carolyn's as it rested on the fork of her saddle.

"What are we waiting for?" Carolyn asked, with stars in her eyes.

The four rode all day, exploring their domain, or part of it, at least, and returned to hobble their horses on the meadow, where their pack horses had already made themselves at home.

"We've just got to build our house near the stream," Carolyn told them, "wouldn't it be fine to be able to hear it day and night?"

"Yes, you couldn't ask for a better place for a home," said Sam as he gazed down at the clear, sparkling stream at their horses' feet.

"We probably don't even have to hobble the horses," Arthur said, "why they'd wander away from a horse heaven like this, I don't know."

"Yes, it's a horse paradise as well as one for humans and cattle," Andrew added, "I just hope it's really available . . . seems too good to be true."

"Tomorrow, I think we'd better start for Las Cruces to file on our homestead," Sam told Carolyn.

He looked at Arthur and Andrew, saying, "Why don't you two try to find some fresh meat? I'll wager you won't need to go very far."

"Why not?" came Arthur's query.

"You see that clump of big trees about two hundred yards up, on the side of the mountain?" Sam pointed directly in front of them toward the hillside. "Well, look closely at the branches; what do you see?"

"Branches!" came Andrew's quick reply. "No, wait, I see them, deer, and there's a buck . . . that rascal thinks the branches are disguising him, and they were, too, with his antlers spread out among the branches. Come on, Arthur, let's get him."

They started off on a circuitous route calculated to prevent startling the buck and a little later, Sam and Carolyn heard one shot as they worked around camp, Sam carrying the packs to a more convenient location, and Carolyn gathering firewood and building a small fireplace out of the plentiful rock.

In a short while, the two brought the deer into camp and began to hang it from a limb, when Sam asked them if they needed any help.

"No, Sam," replied Andrew, busying himself with the buck. When they had enough meat for the evening meal, Arthur carried the venison steaks to Carolyn while Andrew continued to cut up the meat.

"Maybe we'd better cook or smoke some more after supper," he called to the others. "I don't think it's cold enough to hang long without roasting it."

Sam agreed, "Good idea." He was helping Carolyn to rig a spit on which to turn the steaks. "We'll do several roasts tonight, while we have good coals."

He rose to his feet and looked around, "This will be an ideal place for our headquarters," he told the others with satisfaction. "Plenty of water, good shelter, for us and the stock. It's not a weak spring, to judge by the size of the trees around it, so it must run year round. Just look at the wide stretch of green grass around it where it runs through the meadow."

Early the next morning as the sun began to peep over the eastern horizon, all were busy around the camp, preparing for their ride over the mountain and across the Tularosa Basin to Las Cruces, to file their land claims. They had cooked the larger part of the venison and now had it hung high in a pine tree, out of reach of varmints. It was still cold at night in the high country, and the meat should last well. Their supplies were likewise cached out of harm's way, and when Sam asked, "Are we ready to ride?" They responded by swinging into their saddles and making at a trot toward the gap they had ridden through the day before. After awhile they began to climb, their horses picking their way over the rocky trail. They didn't talk much as their horses followed, one behind the other, with Sam in the lead, for each was daydreaming of the future. Carolyn was planning her house, while Sam wondered about the best place to buy cattle, and Andrew and Arthur wondered if there would be any problems at the land office.

Before they realized it, they had reached the base road on the south side of the mountain, and were jerked back to reality by a rider coming toward them.

"Good morning," he called as he looked up at the sun, "or maybe it is early afternoon."

They reined in and returned the polite remarks of the stranger.

"My name is Leandro Sanchez, and I live at Las Tablas on the north side of the mountain."

The others introduced themselves and told of their reason for their trip to Las Cruces.

"We'll be neighbors, then," Leandro told them, "Welcome! Have you been to Las Tablas?"

"Not yet," Carolyn replied, "but we plan to as soon as we get settled."

"Can I be of any help?" Leandro offered.

"As a matter of fact, you can, Senor Sanchez," Sam told him.

"Please," Leandro said, "call me Leandro . . . my father is Senor Sanchez," he continued with a smile.

"All right, Leandro, it is." Sam responded. "We don't know much about the adobe bricks and we do want to build out of them. Can you recommend someone who will be willing to help us when we are ready?"

"I'm considered by many to be one of the best adobe makers in the area. The construction of adobe dwellings is my specialty. I'd be happy to help you build your casa; it would be a privilege."

"Then we are fortunate, indeed," Carolyn told him.

"When can you begin?" Sam asked.

"Today," Leandro answered with a smile. "No, I am just joking. Whenever you are ready, I'll be ready. Just come by Las Tablas when you want me. I won't be hard to find. Everyone knows everyone else there!" He told them goodbye and rode up the trail.

"Now if everyone is as friendly and neighborly as Leandro, we'll be in good shape," Arthur said with satisfaction.

"We're just lucky that Leandro is a good man. Don't hold your breath thinking that all of the rest of the people will be the same," Sam told him. "There are all kinds of people in the world, and this part of it will be no exception."

"I didn't know you were so cynical," Carolyn told her husband, teasingly.

"Guess that's why I became a mountain man," Sam mused. "I like to be alone, away from too many laws, regulations and rules, but that part of our life is over, and I'm sure we'll find good friends here."

CHAPTER XV

They encountered no trouble at the land office. The claims were registered and the legal owners of the land all smiles as they stepped out on to the sidewalk.

"Now it's legal," Carolyn said with a smile as she looked up into Sam's grinning face.

"Yep," Sam told them, "now we have our ranch and we'll have to decide what to call it, what to register as our brand. Do you have any suggestions?"

"How about our initials together, somehow? S slash F or bar F or something similar?" Andrew suggested.

"S-F . . . sounds fine Andrew. What do you two think? He turned to Carolyn and Arthur.

"Let's register it that way, Sam, it sounds just right," Carolyn said, and Arthur agreed.

They continued to talk over their plans as they ate dinner at a small restaurant not far from the land office. They ordered Mexican food, for they were beginning to acquire a taste for the hot, spicy food of the area. Their waitress brought them frijoles, enchiladas, and tortillas, with a side dish of chile verde, and a pot of honey. They relished their food as they ate and Carolyn told them that one of the top priorities was to find out how to prepare such dishes.

"Another top priority is to head for Texas to buy cattle," her husband told her as he helped himself to another tortilla. "Then we can get the house started. Leandro Sanchez probably has men who help him build, and you can oversee the work, Carolyn, tell him what you have in mind, while the rest of us begin work on the outbuildings and corrals."

"Sounds about right to me," said Andrew, as he drank his coffee.

"Let's get started,' Arthur said, "I can't wait to get home."

Their way back led through the Tularosa Basin, that broad valley bordered by mountains, from the Organs and San Andres which join forces on the west to the mighty Sacramento and Sierra Blanca ranges on the east.

As they rode past the eternally shifting white sands, in reality gypsum, they marveled again at their vastness. The huge, white dunes rose high above the surrounding plains.

At the end of the second day, they camped beside the Rio Tularosa and went early to bed.

Their trip back to the north side of their mountain, as they termed it, followed the western side of the Sierra Blancas, home of the Apaches, but their trip proved uneventful, and almost immediately they set forth again, this time on their quest for cattle with which to stock their ranch.

Several days east, they camped beside a windmill and before they left in the morning, the owner of the ranch happened by, greeting them and offering to sell to them all of the cows they needed. He invited them to stay at his ranch house while the cows were gathered. He was an old bachelor and lived alone except for two nephews who helped him ranch. The two boys had survived an Indian attack which had wiped out the rest of the family, some years before that.

When the Sidwell-Fredericks party was ready to move out, the old-timer said that the oldest of the boys had been hankering to see something of the country west of them and told them that he'd be happy to go along with them and help with the cattle.

"He'd be a real help to you, too, until you get used to those critters," the old rancher told them.

"Well, now, we'd sure appreciate having him with us," responded Sam. "There's an awful lot we don't know about ranching and about longhorns in particular, so he'd sure be welcome."

Thus it was that when Sam and the others began their drive home, they had Bill with them. They didn't know it then, but he was to remain for many years an invaluable part of their ranch.

CHAPTER XVI

T en years had passed swiftly, and they had been good years for the Sidwell-Fredricks family. Their herd had thrived and increased, and so had their family.

Sam and Carolyn had two children, Jodie, nine, the oldest, and her brother Ralph, two years younger.

Andrew had married the oldest daughter of the de Vargas family, their neighbor to the west, and Andrea was a lovely addition to their family. Spirited, dark haired, with liquid black eyes, she fitted into the family life at the ranch perfectly.

A beautiful ranch home had been constructed of adobe by the artisan, Leandro Sanchez. It nestled close to the contours of the land not far distant from La Sierra, the mountain. The spring which bubbled and sang as it ran down the hill had been channeled through the house in a stone ditch which widened at the center of the combined kitchen and dining room to a distance of four feet. The crystal clear water flowed year round, a portion of it entering the stone ditch and flowing through the house and out down a small slope, still contained in a stone ditch to a huge stone watering tank for the stock. This tank was located about one hundred yards from the house, and then the overflow made a slow descent down though the grassland and watered a huge old stand of cottonwoods, walnuts, and Ponderosa pines, where many a picnic took place during the long, drowsy months of each year.

The green grass was lush under the trees and cattle could be seen lying in the deep shade during the hottest part of the summer months.

Not far from the water tank were grouped several log buildings, barns, shops, tool sheds, and a long bunk house, all built from logs cut on the ranch. Sam, Andrew, and Arthur had worked hard on the buildings, built one by one whenever the ranch work permitted, and they were good, stout buildings, built to last for generations.

Andrew and Andrea had begun to want a ranch of their own and so they settled on land west of the Rio Grande, in big open country not far from the Tularosa Mountains. During the round-ups, the two ranches were run as one, with the cowhands working both ranges consecutively, during the spring and fall work.

Arthur hadn't married as yet, and had stayed on at the home ranch with Sam and his sister and their children. He had taken to ranching like a duck to water, and Andrew told him that a woman would have an uphill pull to compete with his first love.

Arthur was the innovator, the progressive rancher who watched for new ways to improve the ranch. The admired and respected uncle of his niece and nephew, he always had time to work with them, teaching them how to rope and ride, how to care for the ponies and equipment, how to ride bareback calves in the corral.

As he said, they were going to have a go at it anyway, and he could give them pointers!

He became the last word on what was known to the family as the five W's. When, what, and why to ship, and when and where to brand.

Those ten years hadn't been easy for the S-F ranch. Indian raids, prairie fires, and rustlers had taken their toll, but the uncomplaining mountain men and woman were equal to such hardships, endured them, and finally began to triumph, to leave for their descendants a legacy, a good life, but not an easy one. They typified the breed which later in American history would be known as the undefeatable, immortal cowboy.

They had learned from just which quarter of the ranch they were most apt to expect trouble when it came, as it did periodically. In those far flung sections, the line riders didn't ride alone, but two together, as they rode the outer perimeters of the ranch.

Some riders were dispatched to ride the upper slopes of the mountain, and were thus able to see for long distances, on the lookout for possible trouble. Lincoln County at that time was not the most peaceful place to live, and eternal vigilance was the rule there in order to live and prosper.

The horse herds were especially watched because of the

always present threat from the Apaches and Comanches who needed horses, and delighted in making raids to acquire them.

The Civil War had been fought and the Indians who knew that the forts were undermannned and that the white men fought one another, took to the warpath. The Apaches had pledged themselves to kill or drive every white man from the territory.

That had been the situation one morning as Sam, Arthur, and Ramon Herrera saddled up at the headquarter's corrals. Dust being kicked up down the slope caught their attention and they saw a rider coming at top speed toward them.

"Who's that?" Sam wondered aloud as he continued to cinch up his saddle.

"Manuel," Ramon guessed, "and he's not running like that to bring us good news!"

The three finished saddling and rode out to meet Manuel, who pulled in his horse as he drew near. "Apaches spotted headed toward the horse herd!" He caught his breath as he removed his hat and rubbed his sleeve over his forehead. "A dozen or more of them," he told them.

"Arthur, ride to the cow camp at salt flats, and bring help; Ramon, you and I will ride for the horse herd, and Manuel, you catch up a fresh horse and follow as fast as you can."

A few miles up the mountain in back of the ranch house, three men sat their horses watching the commotion below.

"See, Frank?" One of the riders said as he touched his temple with his gloved finger, "see what can happen when you use your head? We'll wait until that other rider leaves and joins the rest and then we'll pay the missus a visit. A ranch this big must have something of value, maybe gold or a little silver," he said with a laugh. "Those Apaches are good for something. We shouldn't be so mean to them," he grinned.

Carolyn called from the verandah as she watched her husband and the others ride off across the meadow toward an approaching rider, but they hadn't heard her. As she watched, she saw them continue on and the rider trot slowly toward the corrals. She was there to meet him when he reached them. "What's wrong, Manuel?"

"Apaches, senora," came the reply as Manuel dismounted and began to loosen the cinch. "They're after the horses again."

He took down his rope and walked through the corral gate. There were several horses in the corral and he made a neat catch and led the horse back to where his saddle, blanket and bridle lay.

As he quickly saddled and bridled the fresh mount, he told Carolyn what he'd seen, then swung into the saddle and loped away in the direction that Sam and Ramon had taken.

"Be careful," Carolyn called after him and then turned back to the house. When she had gained the verandah, she turned and watched until Manuel was only a speck in the distance.

"Good morning, ma'am," a voice said, and Carolyn turned to see a stranger raising his hat with a sly smile, as he spoke. He and his two companions walked their horses to the foot of the steps and Carolyn could smell trouble just as sure as she had other times when she had act swiftly. Sam had taught her to be calm at times like this and so she eyed the men and their weapons as she looked down on them from the verandah. They sat in a row, and the middle man did the talking while the others just stared.

"We have all the hands we need; we're not hiring. Good day, gentlemen," she said as she turned and walked toward the screen door. She could see Rafaelita behind the curtains just to the left of the door, and she had a pistol in each hand.

"Not so fast," Carolyn heard the spokesman say as she heard him cock the hammer back on his pistol. She stopped at the door when she heard that familiar sound, and slowly turned around with her back nearly touching the door.

"You're not being very friendly," the stranger went on, "this could be painless, or it could be very painful for you, it's your choice."

Carolyn showed no fear as her eyes searched those of the stranger. Only he had his gun drawn, and he handled it carelessly, obviously thinking the situation well in hand. The other two men smiled and one pushed his hat back, eyeing Carolyn's slender form.

"Don't be foolish, lady, just cooperate, and we'll have a little fun and you'll show us where the boss keeps his money box and we'll be on our way. No one will get hurt, all right?"

The three started to dismount. A good time for Rafaelita to act, while their eyes are off me for a second, thought Carolyn. She heard a shot and at the same time she felt a pistol thrust into her hand. The spokesman, with his pistol still in his hand slid slowly from his horse to the ground as Carolyn fired two shots. The other two strangers slumped to the ground as Carolyn placed each of her bullets in the foreheads of the men, a testimony to her accurate shooting. She and Rafaelita ran to the fallen men, pistols at the ready, as they checked to see if they were dead.

"They've crossed over," Carolyn said as she straightened.

Rafaelita looked puzzled through her shock as she asked, "What does that mean?"

"It means," Carolyn said as she touched Rafaelita's arm gently, "that they're dead.";

'Then why don't you say that they're dead, instead of that gringo talk of yours?" Rafaelita asked softly.

"Oh, they're dead," Carolyn said grimly. "And you helped save the day."

"Muchachos, prisa," Rafaelita called as she looked toward the distant barn. Two young boys came running and were instructed to bring some shovels and a pick and she showed them where to dig, and said, "When you have finished, go back to your chores and Senora Sidwell and I will take over."

With expressions of great respect, the two boys turned and ran back to get the required tools.

"Some don't know you yet," Rafaelita told Carolyn, "you would think by now that everyone would know your background and stay away from this ranch." She glanced once more toward the men, and crossed herself as she turned to walk back to the house.

CHAPTER XVII

S am and the others heard the gunfire as they approached Indian Divide draw. They looked at each other as they continued onward and when they had reached the high point of the draw, they could see horses running toward them.

"They're being driven this way," Sam yelled and motioned that they should take cover in some pinons over yonder. The three men reached the trees as the first horse galloped past them, and in seconds the rest of the horses were galloping by them all out, with several Apaches in full pursuit. Both Sam and Ramon fired simultaneously, Manuel a second later, and two of the riders slid from their horses as the others looked to see in what direction the firing originated, at the same time sliding over to the opposite side of their mounts and returning the fire from under their ponies' necks. In minutes, the Indians and horses were disappearing in the distance, the Indians once again sitting astride their ponies.

"Sam," said Ramon, as he gestured, "here come the others."

Riders could be seen coming from the salt flats.

"How many did we lose, Bill?" Sam asked as his ramrod in charge of the horse herd came up to them.

"About thirty head, Sam," Bill Sommers told him. Bill was the young cowboy who had come west with the longhorns years before, and was now in charge of the horse herd, for horses were his first love.

Ten men, armed to the teeth and including Arthur and Bill, now surrounded Sam and the others.

"How bad was it?" asked Arthur.

110

"We got two of them and maybe wounded another," Sam told him.

"Let's go after them!"

Sam turned to one of the riders, "Tim, you go back and tell my wife what we're up to, and stay at headquarters until we get back."

The rest of the men followed Sam and they rode beside the widely trampled trail left by the stampeding horses.

As the sun went behind the hills, they watered their horses at a small stream and Sam studied the tracks, straightened, and told them, "I'd estimate that they're only a few miles ahead of us, by now."

The others concurred, and once more they rode on, at a long trot.

"We must take them tonight," Sam said, "it gives us the advantage of surprise, for they probably don't expect us to follow this close. Also, Apaches don't fight at night, for I've heard that they believe that those who die in battle fighting at night will walk in darkness forever, in that spirit world of theirs. I'll scout ahead," Sam went on, "and Arthur, you follow a little behind, with the men."

An hour after darkness, the men were in the tall pines, their hoofbeats muffled in the dry pine needles which covered the floor of the forest. They moved forward cautiously, as they waited for Sam to backtrack. Suddenly, he loomed up before them, saying, "They're camped not over a mile further on." He beckoned to the men to surround him and went on, softly, "They have one guard out and we'll take care of him. We'll go carefully until we have to go afoot. On my signal, we'll open fire on them. We should be able to get them all."

Sam's signal was that old mountain man yell. He figured the surprise would startle the Indians so they would jump up, looking in the direction from which it had come. That way they would make easy targets.

He had figured well, the startled Indians rose as one man to their feet, looking in the direction of the awful sound. At that moment, the men opened fire. Sam, rifle in hand, charged the camp and within about twenty yards stopped, raised his rifle and began to fire. Some of his men stopped firing and stared at Sam in awe and Bill Sommers grinned and said to Ramon, "Wonder why he brought us along?"

"So we won't forget what we just saw and to leave a message that no one steals from Sam Sidwell and gets away with it." He watched as Sam walked among the fallen Indians, inspecting each one. Ramon then turned to Bill and completed his statement with the words, "I guess."

Sam had found one Apache still alive and one of the Salt Flat boys was about to finish him when Sam said no. The Apache, showing no fear or emotion, wore a streak of yellow paint under each eye. He began his death chant as his eyes stared into Sam's. They didn't blink, nor did he move a muscle, but he continued in that high, then low, variation of his chant, sure that he was about to be killed. It seemed to the cowboy that he was burning a picture of Sam into his brain, that he didn't intend to forget this white man, even in death.

Sam's cold blue eyes met the challenge, and the eyes of the Apache were the first to be averted.

"He's a tough one; let him live," Sam ordered, as he stalked away. "These Apaches are a tough and mean bunch and they know how to raise men who are not afraid to die. They love their country and will resist the white man's encroachment and lifestyle to the death. It's too bad that such courage has to be wasted. One day, I hope, they will see that their ways are over, good or bad, their ways are over."

They gathered the horses and started back, traveling a few miles before they stopped for the night. Around the campfire, built for warmth for they had no food with them, Sam expressed aloud the thoughts he'd been having. "Perhaps the Apaches who survive will give this new nation and people an infusion of their precious courage. Their people may some day live in each of us as we show the world the new breed which we will some day become."

This was a side of Sam seldom seen by his men and most of them were surprised but pleased by his philosophical remarks.

Ramon showed emotion as he agreed with Sam's assessment of the new breed of man, the American. Ramon knew that his conquistador and Castillian blood was already being infused into that new breed. His respect for Sam reached a new plateau because of this small venture into Apacheland. The road would be a bumpy one, he thought, but in the end all of us will be proud to have sacrificed to achieve this end. "Viva America," he muttered, as Bill asked, "What did you say, boss?"

Ramon looked across the flames at Bill and said, as he slapped him on the shoulder, "Nothing, my amigo, nothing. I'm having a wonderful dream."

"My people," Ramon said, as they drove the horses toward

home, "have lived under the eyes of the Apaches for many years, and Sam is right, they are afraid of nothing and will die for their beliefs. When you don't see them is when you should be doubly alert, for they are masters of concealment and can live on almost nothing if they are being pursued."

"Go on, my friend," Bill told him, "these fellows, some of them, haven't had much experience with the Apaches."

"Well," said Ramon, "they've been known to cross the white sands desert and those ignorant enough to try to follow cannot cope with the privations they can endure." He paused to light the cigarette he'd been rolling, and continued, "The Apache will kill and drink the blood of his horse, rather than die of thirst, or he'll kill his horse and fill the large intestine from the horse with water, wrap the intestine around his shoulder and walk into the desert, leaving those foolish enough to follow to die on the desert floor, their bones to bleach in the sun after the buzzards have picked them clean.

"When the Apache is young, he must go through a very difficult training. One such training exercise is the endurance run where he will run a long distance during the hottest season of the year with a mouthful of water and when he reaches the finish line, he must spit the water out, showing he had the stamina and willpower not to drink the water.

"My ancestors, the Spaniards and the Mexicans used to have Indian slave hunts, usually hunting the less warlike tribes such as the Yuma Indians west of here. At certain times of the year, these Indians had a religious fast and when they did not eat for days, they became weak and it was during these fasts that they were captured and sold at the plaza in Santa Fe or at local sales. The Spaniards learned early that the Apaches didn't make good slaves, but the Apaches understood the slave hunts and approved and condoned them because they, themselves, were involved. The Apache believes, truly believes, that he is superior to all other men on earth and he is confident of this superiority. The rest of us, according to the Apache beliefs, have been placed here on earth by the Great Spirit for them to capture and do with us whatever they wish.

"And if you ever see an Apache woman with her nose cut off, or rather the end of it, it is a sign that she was an adulteress, an unfaithful wife, and has been marked for life as a reminder to all other Apache women of the fate of those who disobey and defy tribal law."

Those riding near Ramon found his words enlightening, for many of the young cowboys had come from other areas of the country, remote from the customs and habits of the Apaches.

"They're good fighters, all right," said Bill, "they can match us in courage and dedication."

"They surpass most of us in those areas," Ramon went on, "believe me, the Apaches roam everywhere, undefeated, usually in war parties, not over ten or twenty strong, though known to number as high as two hundred. Our catching them the way we did is unusual, you know. When pursued, they usually scatter like straw in the wind, usually having extra horses where they can change, leaving the pursuers on tired horses. This little band were young, mostly untried, or they'd never have been caught. If the truth were written they outsmarted, and outfought the Spaniards, then the Mexicans, and now the Americans.

"When they have a council, for any reason, all may speak, even the women who may also go on war parties if they choose . . ."

Sam rode up beside Ramon and asked, "What are you up to, old friend? You're teaching again, aren't you? You were born too soon . . . you would be, and are, one hell of a teacher. I hope these boys are taking in your lessons; it might save their lives some day!" He rode on, then looked back and yelled, "Listen to him, boys."

"The Apache travels a lot lighter than his opponents. A light bridle or rope and a light pad or saddle make up his trappings."

"Do all Apaches dress alike, Ramon?"

"No, the Jicarillas who live in the northern part of New Mexico Territory resemble the plains Indians with their buckskin clothing and braided hair, while the Mescaleros let their hair grow long and straight, holding it back with a headband. They wear high leggings and long tunics over their breech clouts." He paused, looking around at the engrossed faces of the young riders. "Have you had enough? No? Well, I'll just tell you a little more and then stop! Did you know that when the Apaches return from a raid, there is a victory celebration and all of the warriors who died in battle are mentioned with honor, but never again? If a dead warrior's name is mentioned thereafter, it can summon him from the hereafter and can bring down his wrath.

"These things are not written because the Apaches have no written language, but depend upon their history being handed down by word of mouth from generation to generation. Also, the Apaches don't take scalps as do most Indians, and they seldom smoke the peace pipe."

"Doesn't sound as though they're after peace anyway," observed one of the young cowboys.

When they drove the horses into the pens at headquarters later that day, the men unsaddled and turned their mounts into another corral, throwing feed to them all. The care of the animals first, a strict rule at the ranch, was not to be ignored if one wanted to keep working at the S-F.

Sam, Arthur, and Ramon walked up the front steps of the house as Carolyn and Rafaelita went to meet them. "Did you lose any men?" was Carolyn's first question, and then, "did you get the horses back?" her second as she reached up to receive Sam's kiss and hug. Rafaelita also received a hearty hug from her husband, and watching them, Arthur thought it might not be a bad thing to be married and receive such a warm welcome when he returned, as they did.

They told the women about their chase after the horses as they went toward the kitchen and Carolyn said, "I'll bet you're famished! We'll just get something to put into those stomachs of yours while you tell us about it."

After they'd eaten, the three men went out to the verandah to smoke while they discussed ranch work.

"When do you think those . . .?" Arthur broke off as he noticed the horse tracks which came around the house, tracks where they never rode. He stood up and walked down the steps and over to where the tracks were, stooping to examine them closely. "Not very old," he said back over his shoulder. By this time Ramon and Sam had joined him to examine the tracks which led from behind the house. "Someone was here while we were gone," Sam told them. "Let's ask the girls."

"They were strangers looking for trouble," Carolyn said from the top of the stairs.

Rafaelita came out of the house, drying her hands on her apron as Carolyn began to tell what happened. "We buried them on the other side of that arroyo," Rafaelita put in as Carolyn seemed to be finished.

"Guess we don't have to worry about our womenfolk, do we Ramon?" Sam said, but Carolyn knew that her news had disturbed him more than he admitted.

"The Apaches aren't the only enemy to fear now," Ramon told his wife as he hugged her to him, "more and more outlaws are coming into this area. Your practice with the pistol paid off, my querida, even though you hated to take the time to do it."

They were still digesting this bit of news, when Sam noticed a rider headed their way. "At least he's not in too big a hurry, so maybe it's not bad news."

They recognized the buckskin which was a favorite mount of their neighbor to the east, Senor Sisneros.

"Welcome, Senor!" called Sam as their neighbor dismounted and tied his horse to the long hitching rack.

Fernando shook hands with the others as he reached the porch, and tipped his hat to Carolyn and Rafaelita.

"Querer cerveza, Senor?" Rafaelita asked.

"Por favor," Fernando answered with a smile as he sat down with the others. "Well, Sam, I bring news about the war back east; it was back east," he amended.

"What do you mean, was?" questioned Sam.

"An army of Texans, under the Confederate flag have just taken Fort Bliss at El Paso and also Fort Fillmore at Mesilla and the word is that they're on their way to Fort Stanton."

"What do they want in New Mexico?" asked Arthur.

"Gold," Senor Sisneros told them grimly.

"What gold? There's not that much gold here," Arthur put in.

"You're quite right, my friend, but California with her gold will be theirs, if they can cut California off from the rest of the country by taking New Mexico Territory. As you know, the war is going badly for the Confederates, and it is their belief that with the California gold, they can purchase war materials which can make the difference."

"Two riders coming from the west," Ramon interrupted.

As the two men rode up to the house, one of them swung off his horse and strode up the walk to the steps of the verandah. "Fort Stanton is being abandoned," he told them, "lock, stock and barrel . . . what they can't take with them, they're destroying."

"Which way are the troops headed?" Sam asked him.

"North," came the reply.

"Probably toward Santa Fe," Sam said, "they probably think they haven't the force to hold out against the Confederates here. What do you say we ride over to La Placita to find out what else we can? We'd better wait till tomorrow, however."

He turned back to the rider, "Chris, you had better ride to all of the line camps and tell them to be doubly alert for rustlers or strangers of any kind and especially for Indians. And Jay, you round up a few men to stay here at headquarters until we get back."

116

He turned to Senor Sisneros, "Will you stay here for the night and go with us to La Placita, or do you have to get back home?"

"I'll stay the night, senor, gracias," his neighbor told him. "I'd like to ride to La Placita with you."

He declined the meal which Carolyn offered to prepare and so, a little later, she and Rafaelita brought sandwiches, coffee, and thick wedges of pie to the long living room where the men sat before the fire.

Carolyn was proud of her living room with its many windows to the south, the massive stone fireplace at one end of the room, and the bookshelves which lined two of the walls. Her parents had left their extensive library with a brother in the east when they began their trek to Oregon, and so Carolyn had had it shipped out to her and her brothers within the last year, and it had been like greeting old friends to take the books from the boxes and place them on the shelves which Sam had made for them.

As she dropped into a chair, she glanced around the room lovingly. The roughly plastered adobe walls were painted white and the walls shone in the firelight. The wide plank floor was strewn with Navajo rugs and saddle blankets. It was a peaceful, yet colorful room, a place to relax, or read, or visit with their neighbors. The distances were far to travel, and when neighbors came to call, they stayed a while, for they didn't see each other often.

She listened to the men talking, to Senor Sisneros telling the others that he fully expected that the renegade Apaches would take to the warpath once more as a result of the abandonment of the fort.

"Like the ones who tried to run off our horses," Arthur told him, "and it's not fair that we blame all of them for the depredations of a few, but we do."

"No, it may not be fair, but it's been true down through the ages, and will continue," their neighbor pointed out. "I read in the *Las Vegas Optic* newspaper the last time I was there, that some rustlers had teamed up with a sheepherder to rustle sheep belonging to Roberto Sisneros, no relation as far as I know. The rustlers turned the chuck wagon over and tore the thing apart and then the sheepherder and one of the rustlers went at it to make it look as though the herder had defended his flock as much as he dared. They knew the rancher would be there that day to check the flock and when he got there, the herder could blame the Indians. The rancher was fooled for a while."

"An ingenious way to rustle," Arthur said, "if you can get

away with it, and apparently some of them succeed."

In the morning, the four set out for the little village, heading for the Gap Road at a trot. Sam and Fernando rode together with Ramon and Arthur just behind. As they climbed through the gap, Ramon began to sing softly in Spanish. Sam and Fernando carried on their conversation, but Arthur was listening to the words of Ramon's song, and finally questioned him about it.

"It's an old Spanish ballad about a violin player who lived up in Belen, up close to Albuquerque, in the old days," Ramon said.

"Sounds pretty, why don't you sing it a little louder? I'd like to hear it."

Ramon raised his voice a little as he continued with the song.

"It would sound much better if Ramon had a guitar," Fernando Sisneros said as he turned in his saddle and glanced back approvingly. "We have many old ballads, many of them very sad, which we have had handed down to us."

Ramon's ballad told the story of the violin player who was said to be the finest player in upper New Spain. A wedding was to take place in Las Vegas and Vicente was employed to play at the wedding festivities. During his absence from home, the Comanches made a raid on Belen, and his wife and children were taken prisoners. When he returned to Belen, he couldn't accept the fate which others of the small village took so philosophically, that it was a sad fact of life. They told him that he couldn't possibly expect to get his family back, but he wouldn't listen and saddled his horse once more and taking a pack horse, he headed for the plains of Texas, never to be seen again.

So thought the people of Belen. Many watched him as he disappeared over the horizon and the black shawled women had crossed themselves, murmuring short prayers for the poor soul. May God help him.!

After many months of searching, Vicente came to a Comanche camp where he found his family. But his wife had married a chief and had a child by him. The ballad never says with whom she went, Vicente or her Comanche husband. It was her choice to make and the song ends leaving the listener to wonder whom she finally chose.

As the men reached the summit of the gap, they pulled their horses in to rest and gazed at the smoke coming from the vicinity of the fort.

"They must have set fire to it, not wanting to leave anything for the Confederates," said Sam, breaking the silence. The smoke was drifting slowly eastward on a slight breeze, and the men could imagine the desolation. But the stone stables would be there, yet.

"A beautiful location for a fort," Ramon mused, breaking the silence yet again.

The four men rode down the trail to the Base Road and turned eastward, toward La Placita.

"The Torreon will be kept busy as the Apaches increase their raids," Arthur commented, as he glanced behind them.

"What's the matter?" asked Ramon.

"Nothing, I just thought I saw something out of the corner of my eye. Probably a deer, or maybe an elk."

"Be alert," Fernando said, with a somber expression.

As they approached the outskirts of La Placita, they were halted by a procession of Penitentes, dressed in robes of Franciscan appearance. The procession was winding up the hill toward the Penitente cemetery. They chanted a religious song as they progressed on their pilgrimage.

They waited, holding their hats, until the procession had passed around the curve of the hill before Sam said, softly, "I'd heard of that, but never saw it before."

"I'll tell you about it some other time, my friend," Fernando told him, as they continued down the north side of the Rio Bonito. They splashed across the shallow river and came into La Placita and Sam suggested they go to Tito's cantina down the street beyond the Torreon. They tied their mounts to the rack in front of the little cantina and entered. Tito greeted them with a smile and a handshake, saying, "Como esta usted, mi amigos." (How do you do, my friends.)

"Muy bien, gracias, usted," (Very well, thank you.) They all answered, almost in unison.

"Cerveza, por favor," Fernando told him.

"Bien," Tito replied as he turned back to the counter.

Just as Sam started to ask Tito what he'd heard about the fort, they could hear the sounds of galloping horses and shooting in the street. Dust wafted through the open door and shouting was heard as the riders hitched their horses at the rack. An occasional shot was heard as they continued to fire into the air, or near any unfortunate individual who happened to be in the vicinity. A stranger clanked into the cantina, his spur straps let out to the 'town hole' as they called it, a way of proclaiming to the townspeople that cowboys were in town, often indulged in by the younger riders. Apparently Tito's was not his first stop, for he fired three rounds at a whiskey bottle uncomfortably close to Tito's head. He stopped shooting and glanced at the men seated around one of the tables. He holstered his gun and kindly advised them to stay out of the way, for he and his outfit intended taking over the town for a while.

Arthur rose, facing the stranger as he said softly, "What if we don't?"

"You don't hear so good, do you cowboy? I said to stay out of my way!" He was drawing his pistol as he spoke, but before he could pull it clear of the holster, Arthur had drawn and fired, and the stranger doubled over, falling to the floor.

"He's one of the Seven Rivers gang, I believe," Tito said as he inspected the man. "He's dead," he continued, as he looked up at the others from his kneeling position. "They're no good, those hombres. They picked today to make a visit to La Placita because the sheriff is out of town."

Shots could be heard once more in the street, but this time many more guns were involved.

"Jose Montano and the San Patricio men, I'll bet," Tito yelled, as he ran to the small window and peered out.

"Who in hell is Jose Montano?" shouted Sam.

"The leader of a bunch of San Patricio riflemen who protect the people in times like these. Someone must have spotted the rustlers as they came through Hondo or San Patricio and told Jose," Tito surmised.

The battle, if it could be called that, was over almost immediately as the outlaws from Seven Rivers recognized the superior fire power and left the village on a high lope, encouraged by the native riflemen, who chased them well past Las Chozas before they turned back.

As the shooting faded into the distance, the street once more became filled with people. Some of them came into the cantina to have a drink and discuss the shooting.

"Another Valverde," Carlos Salcido said with a laugh, as he sat down at a table not far from the north siders.

"What happened at Valverde?" Fernando asked him.

Carlos turned to Fernando, shook hands and said, "You didn't hear about that battle, Senor Sisneros?"

"No, please, you and your friend join us at our table and tell us about it."

After introducing everyone, Carlos continued, telling of how the soldiers at Fort Fillmore on the Rio Grande, left their fort before the Confederates arrived. "I guess the commander thought he could join forces with the soldiers here at Fort Stanton, and make a stand here, but some smart Confederate sympathizer, I hear, convinced the Union enlisted men to fill their canteens with whiskey instead of water, as they had been ordered to do. Now the whiskey was to have been destroyed along with everything else, but the troopers weren't about to pour good whiskey on the ground!

"Well, anyway, halfway across the White Sands, they were all drunk, and with no trouble the Texas Confederates captured them. I guess that's why our friends at Fort Stanton thought it was the better part of valor just to high tail it up north."

Carlos took a long drink of beer and continued, "The next time the Confederates and Union boys met it was at Valverde, just south of Socorro. Fort Craig is near there, as you know. The boys in blue outnumbered those Confederates by about a thousand men and when the Confederates tried to cross the Rio Grande, the Union boys stopped them. Then the Union tried to cross the river to defeat the rebs and those southern boys must have loved their cause more than that Union bunch under Governor Connelly, who was convinced he could win. Anyway, when Connelly's men crossed the river to mix it up with the Texans, they walked into a regular rattlesnake's nest. The Confederates threw everything at them as they charged the boys in blue. You know, those grey boys used double barreled shotguns at close quarters, with such skill that those Union boys still can't figure out what happened. In six hours the Confederates had taken the field and the Union men began to retreat toward Santa Fe, leaving Albuquerque to the Confederates too. I wouldn't be surprised if Connelly doesn't desert Santa Fe and retreat on to Fort Union, or the boys from Fort Union might meet Connolly at Las Vegas. I hear the Colorado militia are on their way to help. "That's where the war is at this point," Carlos concluded, as he took another swallow of beer.

They sat silently for a time, digesting this fund of information, then thanked Carlos, paid for another round for him and his friend, and left the cantina.

"There's more to come, and let's hope it doesn't spill over into our area or into Andrew's," Ramon muttered as he gathered his reins, stuck his toe into his stirrup and swung into the saddle.

"Well, we came to the right place to find out the news," commented Sam dryly, as he and others mounted and retraced their steps out of the little village.

"They weren't too far from Andrew for awhile there," said Arthur, "I suppose he's heard about it by now also."

The next news they heard came from their neighbor to the west, Juan de Vargas, Andrea's father, who told them the Confederates had been driven out of New Mexico after they suffered a defeat at Glorieta, just east of Santa Fe, and delivered by the combined forces of the Union, the New Mexico militia, and the Colorado Volunteers. A column had been on the way from California, but hadn't arrived in time. However, it had stayed on to help with the Indian trouble.

De Vargas went on, telling Carolyn and Sam about the news he had heard while he drank coffee with them in the large sunny kitchen of the ranch house.

"However, I think Connelly is going about that problem in the wrong way," he told the Sidwells worriedly. "He's showing no mercy toward the Indians and he has ordered all Indians to either be killed or placed on reservations. A reservation about forty miles square has been established at Fort Sumner, on the Pecos River. General Carleton's order to Governor Connelly was to the effect 'that all men of the Mescalero tribe were to be killed wherever and whenever they were found, that it was too late to make peace with the white men and that they were to be soundly whipped without parley or council'.

"From what I hear, Kit Carson has been put in charge of bringing the Navajos to their knees, starved into submitting to life on a reservation. This is to be done by destroying their crops, and their orchards, and I've heard that they were ordered to report to the Bosque Redondo Reservation no later than July 20, 1863."

De Vargas rose, walked to the kitchen window as he sipped his coffee and looked toward the horizon, "Too many changes, Sam, too many changes, I guess I'm getting old; I don't like them."

"I, too, feel the same, old friend, but we must be prepared to be good neighbors to the good people and ready to protect our outfits from those not so good," Sam told him as they walked out the back door and around the house.

"There will be a lot of bad hombres being driven out of the neighboring states as well as territories," said de Vargas. "The Texas and Arizona rangers are responsible for that, and I don't blame them, but we're going to reap the benefits," said Sam's neighbor with a grim smile of farewell.

"He's right, honey," Sam told his wife later, "we're going to be in for some years of turmoil before it's over. A lot of unsavory

122

characters like those you and Rafaelita disposed of are going to be coming through these parts." He put his arms around his wife and gathered her to him, "Be very careful, my dear, when you're anywhere on the ranch. Don't know what I'd do if anything happened to you. I still remember how lost Andy Jackson was without his Rachel, and we have a marriage like that, Carolyn, the very best."

Carolyn brushed his cheek with the back of her hand as she hugged him close to her and then kissed him.

"Maybe we'd better go armed when we're out away from the house at all, Sam. Remember, we used to do so all the time. If it hadn't been for Rafaelita that day it could have turned out far differently when those men threatened us."

"Sisneros, de Vargas, and we had better work more closely together than we have been already," Sam mused. "I'm going to suggest that maybe we can work out a plan to constantly patrol the three spreads, working together. It won't hurt to talk it over, anyway."

A little later, Carolyn brought a tray of sandwiches and coffee to the verandah, placing them on a small table near the chairs. As her husband joined her, she reminded him, "Whatever happens, we can handle it, honey, as long as we are together, we can handle any problem. We have each other, the children, Arthur, Ramon and Rafaelita, and the cowboys, and if we add the Sisneros and de Vargas outfits to that, we'll have a formidable front for anyone to crack."

Sam reached out to pat Carolyn's knee as he said, "Yes, you're right, my dear, as long as we're together we're undefeatable, just as a bunch of pencils is more difficult to break than each one individually. What do you say we saddle up early tomorrow and pay a visit to our neighbor to the east, John Chisum?"

Rafaelita had food packed for them and was stowing it away into the saddle bags when the two walked into the kitchen. Carolyn wore the new style of riding pants called levis, the first time she had tried them, as usually she wore the divided skirt which came well below her boot tops. She liked the new pants, and Sam complimented her on how trim she looked. Sam's levis showed signs of long wear, for they were faded to a much lighter color than Carolyn's. It was a long standing joke that a stranger could tell the married men from the bachelors just by looking at the color of their levis. The pants the married men wore received regular washing and were faded as a result, while the single men were apt to take a casual attitude in that respect.

Carolyn and Sam both wore side arms and were carrying rifles to place in their saddle scabbards. And indeed, there had been very few times since they had settled in the territory that they hadn't felt compelled to go armed.

Rafaelita smiled as she looked at the bowie attached to the left side of Carolyn's belt. "I hope that the people you two meet will have the good sense to ride on by and not take a notion to challenge you!"

"We hope so, too," Carolyn said as she smiled back at Rafaelita and said, "what would we do without you, Rafaelita? You are the sister I never had."

Sam and Carolyn rode away from the ranch house, welcoming the chance for a long talk, for many times their work took them in opposite directions. So, as they rode, they talked of old times, of how they had met, the years they had spent trapping and the good times and bad they had lived through while building their ranch.

"Jodie and Ralph must not forget their heritage. They will be lesser people if they don't remember and cherish the remembrance of those who have gone before them," Carolyn told her husband.

He agreed, "Why don't we begin to write it down when we get back? They may not be interested now, but they will be some day and be glad we did it." He pointed to his left, "Riders, two of them."

"It's the kids," Carolyn said a little later.

"Don't let them hear you say that," Sam said, smiling at his wife. "They feel very grown up now, as they keep reminding us."

"Everything all right?" Carolyn greeted them as their children rode up to them.

"Where are you headed?" Ralph asked as he reined in beside them.

"To visit Mr. Chisum. Everything all right at the line camp?"

"Fine," Jodie replied, "but I wish I were a boy instead of a girl. I could get along better with the cowboys. They pamper me too much and don't want me to do anything by myself."

"Well, we can't change that," her mother told her with a smile, "you'll have to learn to live with the fact that you're a girl which shouldn't prevent you from becoming a successful ranch-woman, unless you let it!"

"Watch the ranch while we're away, but don't ride alone, and be sure to go armed when you're out. We may be away for a few days so don't worry if we don't come right back," their father instructed them.

They separated, riding in different directions, and Jodie called back after they had ridden a little way, "I love you!"

Sam and Carolyn looked back, smiling and waving, "We love you!"

"We're so very lucky to have such fine children," Carolyn sighed.

"No luck about it . . . look at their parents," Sam grinned, but then continued with a more sober expression, "that's why decent people must make sure that their children have a chance for a good life; why the lawless element must be stamped out. Each generation had to do its share and it's time our generation got organized and did its.

"That's one reason I wanted to talk with John Chisum, would like to hear his views. I'll bet he's suffered some pretty heavy losses in cattle and horses already. The no-goods must be stopped, for they make a living from the misery of others. It happens over and over again until the good people decide they've had enough and band together to put a stop to it.

"I've reached that point now, and I think we should begin to fight back. Everyone may not have reached that point, but someone has to start somewhere, must make a beginning.

"Putting a stop to the Apache problem is something else; a lot of bad water has flowed under the bridge and there's too much bad feeling between the Indians and the white man's government and its representatives. It's been said that history repeats itself over and over and people vote the worst elements of mankind into office or promote the most opportunistic, heartless scavengers to high offices. The ancient Greeks called them tyrants and demagogues. Old Andy Jackson knew it, and talked to me about it.

"Take the Indian question, as an example. We've lied and cheated them, never making any effort to understand them or their culture, assuming that they're subhuman creatures, fit only to be exterminated, eradicated, in a way deplorable to anyone with a sense of human compassion. If we had treated them fairly from the beginning, much of the Indian problem might have been averted. We've been guilty of many of the things we've deplored in them. It's time we examined our treatment of them and tried to make amends. And we should always remember that we've blamed all Indians for the actions of a few. And not all white men have condoned our mishandling of the Indian situtation; that, too, has been done by a minority of the whites, but no doubt the Indians blame all of us.

"Probably a majority of the Apaches are law-abiding even though much which they cherish has been destroyed by us. Some of them have refused to change their way of living, preferring to die rather than abandon their customs. It is these whom the white man terms savage renegades, maddened beyond reason, who must be eradicated."

"When a white man takes up rustling, all white men are not blamed, so why do we tend to classify all Indians together?" asked Carolyn.

"I guess if I were an Indian, I'd be a renegade," reflected Sam.

"Then I'd be one of the women warriors!" Carolyn told him, her eyes twinkling.

"Remember the story we heard, Carolyn, about the Indian who watched the white men killing a young buffalo for supper? The white men expected trouble from the Indian and kept an eye on him, but he figured that if the white needed food, it was all right if he killed the buffalo for meat. By the same token, he expected to be able to kill a cow for the same reason, with impunity, and it doesn't always work that way."

"Let's hope we don't abuse our new citizens, the Mexicans, as some of us have done the Indians," Carolyn said fervently.

"Guess we'd better start looking for a likely place to camp," Sam said some time later, "I hope I haven't been boring you with what I've had on my mind, honey."

"Don't apologise, Sam, I want to know what you're thinking, just as I expect to share my thoughts with you. Before I met you, I knew nothing about the Indians and the West. Back in Derry, New Hampshire, life is a lot different than it is out here, believe me. And yet at one time, the early settlers there had similar hardships to contend with, including Indians."

"We're almost to the eastern end of La Sierra, and we'll soon be in the rolling, high plains, so why not set up camp near the foot of the mountain?" Sam suggested.

"Fine with me, but why not go a little farther and camp by that small stream up ahead?" Carolyn said.

"What stream?" Sam asked with a smile. He knew that Carolyn was right and even though the stream couldn't be seen, it had to be there or the trees wouldn't be so huge.

The water at the spring was icy and the grass was thick and green under the trees where they unsaddled and hobbled their horses. The air was chill for the sun had gone behind the mountain and they built a small fire for warmth, as well as for the coffee they made to go with the food which Rafaelita had prepared.

Sam rose and brought their saddles closer to the fire to use as pillows while Carolyn placed their rifles and pistols nearby, and unrolled their blankets. The inside of the sheeplined skirts of their saddles made a fine pillow for each of them.

The fire had died down and they could see the starry sky spread out over them as they lay warm and snug.

"They say that John Chisum sleeps on two blankets and it makes no difference where he is, out on the range or in the house. No bed for him, just two blankets on the ground or floor. I've also heard he carries no arms. Because he's not fast with a gun, and if he were armed, sooner or later he'd get called, so he goes unarmed, but not unprotected, for he has armed gunmen with him wherever he goes," Sam said as he thought of the man they were to visit the next day.

"Guess we'd better try to go to sleep," Carolyn said drowsily as she raised on one elbow to see if her pistol, rifle, and bowie were where she could reach them with no difficulty. Sam watched approvingly, smiling.

It was dark as pitch; heavy rain clouds had blown in, covering the moon, when they awoke, wondering what had disturbed them. Certainly something had bothered them, and they felt chagrined that their senses hadn't been more alert. Why hadn't they awakened sooner, before the danger, whatever it was, was so near? They both sensed the same thing, however, there were four men out there. They each hoped the other knew this, as their eyes searched the darkness and they slowly reached for their weapons. A click was heard and a voice told them, "I wouldn't do that if I were you." As their eyes became accustomed to the thick, soft darkness, they could see the figures of two men before them. They stared down at Sam and Carolyn and they each had a pistol trained on them. "People who poke their noses where they're not wanted get them shot off," one of them confided.

"What in hell are you talking about?" Sam asked. "We don't even know who you are."

As the two men seemed about to fire, two shots rang out and Sam and Carolyn thought they were their crossing papers. But neither was hit. They looked quickly at each other and then back at the men, seeing them sink to the ground. Behind them, the bushes rustled and they leaped to their feet, scooping up their rifles, and then Caroyn shouted, "Thor!" Sam yelled, "Lone Wolf!" Carolyn hugged Thor as Sam pumped Lone Wolf's hand.

"They're not alone," Thor told them, "there's at least three more of them back there, getting ready to rustle some cattle. I hope they're not yours?"

"Probably Chisum's cattle," Sam told him, "wonder where his riders are."

"Don't know, but these boys have a good sized bunch corraled a couple of miles from here in a little canon. What do you bet they have a buyer lined up?" Lone Wolf grinned.

"Feel up to getting those rascals?" Thor asked Sam and Carolyn with a chuckle, "or are you getting too civilized by your fancy living?"

They walked the last quarter of a mile on foot, taking great care not to make any noise on the rocky ground. Lone Wolf pointed out the dim figures of three riders who were stationed at strategic points at the mouth of the canon. He pointed to the one farthest away and pointed to himself and ran his finger across his throat, signifying he'd get that one. Thor pointed to another and then to Sam, and then to the last one and touched his own chest. "You keep yourself in reserve," he whispered to Carolyn.

Lone Wolf acted with speed as the rustler slid from his saddle with a knife in his back.

"What happened to Tom . . .?" another started to ask as he felt Thor's heavy bowie sinking into his back. The third rustler heard the brush move as Sam knocked him from the saddle, and bound him hand and foot.

The sun was coming over the horizon as the four dead rustlers were strapped across their saddles and the other helped to mount because his hands were tied behind his back.

"Where shall we take these no-goods?" Thor inquired of Sam.

"We'll take them to the owner of the cattle, who lives less than a day's ride from here," replied Sam as he tightened his cinch and threw a rein around his horse's neck. "Carolyn and I were on our way to see him anyway, and so we'll just deliver these rustlers to him as a calling card, have a short palaver and start for home." He grinned at his friends, "Jodie and Ralph will sure be glad to meet you two!''

"What do you say to that, Lone Wolf?" Thor asked his friend.

"I don't have anything else to do today," he answered with a broad smile.

The rustler sat his horse with a smug smile on his face. Lone Wolf glanced at him, winked at Sam, and pulled his bowie from its sheath. He reined his horse toward the rustler, saying, "This one could give us some trouble, so I'll just fix it so that he'll ride the rest of the way in the same fashion as his friends back there!"

"Suit yourself," Sam told him.

"You can't let him kill me in cold blood," the rustler yelled, fear showing in his eyes and his face sweating.

"Lone Wolf," Sam suggested, "Carolyn is out of practice, why don't you let her finish this hombre off?"

Carolyn pulled her bowie and threw it at a nearby tree. It sank into the soft pine about an inch.

"Carolyn," Lone Wolf chided her, "this civilized living has almost ruined you. I've seen you do a lot better than that. Remember when you hacked off that thieving redskin's nose up on the Snake River? That redskin didn't think a woman would do that, and he thought it was just luck till you hacked off both ears with two more throws."

The rustler was staring at Carolyn with horrified fascination, and missed Lone Wolf's grin.

"You sure made a believer out of him and you couldn't have manufactured a more fitting punishment for an Indian. A squaw marking him up like that. He couldn't go back to his tribe after that. Do you think you can repeat the feat, Carolyn, on this here fellow?"

"Please," the rustler told them, "it wasn't my idea to run off that stock . . . they talked me into it," he nodded toward the dead men.

"You're not going to get a contradiction from them," Sam told him grimly. "We'll let the owner decide."

It was near dusk when they approached the Chisum headquarters, not far from the Pecos River. Four men came out of the house when the S-F riders were still some distance away. Three of them stood perhaps a pace behind the fourth, who Sam figured was John Chisum.

"Howdy," Sam said, as he pulled his horse in about thirty feet from the porch where the men stood. The man he judged to be Chisum answered, "Howdy," in return. Sam and the rest of his party had looked the place over carefully as they rode in and now Chisum asked, "Where did you get the baggage?"

"Would you be John Chisum?" Sam asked as he dismounted. Carolyn and the others remained where they were.

"That's correct; I'm John Chisum. What can I do for you?"

"Then I guess this baggage is yours, then, plus this live one." Sam walked up to Chisum and extended his hand as he said, "I'm Sam Sidwell of the S-F, north of La Sierra, and this is my wife, Carolyn. The buckskin men are my friends, Thor Elkinson and Lone Wolf McClan."

"Pleased to make your acquaintance, ma'am," Chisum tipped his hat to Carolyn and shook hands with the men, "been wanting to meet my neighbors."

"These men were helping themselves to some of your cattle, and to make a long story short, we had a fuss, and only that one there," Sam pointed to the rustler, "was lucky enough to make it here in one piece."

John Chisum introduced the men who were with him and then said, "Ted, take care of all of them."

"Right, Mr. Chisum." He and one of the others took the reins of the laden horses and as well as that of the remaining rider, and led them away. "Who in hell are those people? Never saw them before, and never want to see them again," they heard the rustler tell the Chisum men.

"Come on into the house," Chisum issued the invitation heartily. He turned back to his foreman and instructed that their horses be seen to, then led the way inside. "You'll stay for supper."

During the meal, they learned that Chisum came from Tennessee also, from Madison County. He had acquired a number of ranches over the territory, mainly the southeastern portion, and it was said that he ran about eighty thousand cows and employed close to a hundred cowboys, but that was his business, and men didn't question one another as to their holdings, or as a matter of fact, about much else. Their business was their own.

During the evening meal and the long talk afterward, they found that Chisum shared their concern about the lawlessness. He also figured it could lead to open warfare over government beef contracts. The signs all pointed to it.

As Sam told them, "If you can read one kind of sign, the chances are you can read another kind, and I think I've read it right in this case. We all need to be on the lookout for trouble."

John Chisum agreed, "It looks as though the different factions are jockeying for position to frame or destroy the others for profit. The greed is extending as far as Santa Fe and beyond, to Washington, D.C. And the Indian is going to be on the short end of the stick."

"It's good to know that you see that too, John," Sam told him, "it looks like that to us, and it's time we dealt squarely with the Indians. It's the only way we'll have peace in the long run, and it's the right thing to do."

"Yes, we've done a lot of things which were expedient, but not always the right thing," conceded Chisum.

Sam and Carolyn and the others discussed further the troubled times as they rode back toward their ranch after breakfast the following morning.

"Old Andy Jackson told me how hard it is to fight crooked politicians, even though you're one hundred percent right, and they're dead wrong," Sam mused, "but if you're a man, sooner or later, you have to stand up and fight for what you believe."

"You're the same old Sam!" Thor said heartily, clapping his friend on the back. "If we stand up to them from the beginning, they may reason that it's in their best interest to let us be. The only thing that kind of jasper understands is power and force, so if we respond in kind, they'll get the message. And I do mean we, for we're cuttin' ourselves in on this, aren't we?" He grinned at Lone Wolf.

Lone Wolf grinned back contentedly, "We all have to leave this earth some day, and what better way than getting rid of rattlesnakes?"

"We may not come to that," laughed Sam, "but we couldn't have anyone siding with us better than you two, if it does come to a showdown. That'll give us an excuse to keep you here for a while, won't it, Carolyn?"

"They know we'd like for them to stay from now on," responded Carolyn, smiling at their good friends.

"You can count on us in a showdown," Lone Wolf said, "sometimes I think I've lived too long . . . things are changing for the worse, with squatters everywhere plowing up grazing land in places never meant to be farm land. They stay awhile, fighting a losing battle, then move on broke, and a little smarter, I hope. But it will take years for that land to come back to growing grass instead of weeds. And they wonder why the Indian goes on the warpath.''

"There were no people more free than the mountain men, on this good earth,'' said Thor, "but that era is over now. That is why Lone Wolf and I have come, to spend our last days with our good friends. Kinda thought if you didn't mind, we'd build a cabin in the forest on your ranch and as payment, you'd know we were handy in a scrap.''

"You're handy in a scrap . . . and that's for sure!'' Sam shook Thor's hand and then that of Lone Wolf. "And your help may be needed more often than you think!''

CHAPTER XVIII

The rays of the rising sun cast long shadows from the barns and corrals, shadows which stretched toward the big house of the S-F Ranch. Suddenly, the screen door opened and Sam, Lone Wolf and Thor stepped out onto the verandah. Each carried a filled coffee cup and they walked to a circular table which was a few feet to the left of the door. The men could hear the soft voices and the laughter of the women as they cleared the table of the breakfast dishes. The deeper sound of Ralph's voice as he teased his mother and sister could be heard also.

"I like the sound of Lincoln. It was a good choice for the name to replace La Placita," Sam commented as he sat down and placed his cup on the table.

"President Lincoln would have been proud to know, had he lived, that the largest county in the territory as well as the town were named in his honor," Thor concurred.

Lone Wolf suggested wryly, "But if he had lived, they might not have been named after him at all." He watched a rider coming at top speed up through the pasture. "Who do you suppose that is?" He nodded in that direction.

The three men rose and walked to the railing of the verandah and Ralph joined them as they waited for the approaching horseman.

"It looks like Ramon," Sam finally decided.

"It is," Thor agreed, "I can make out that blaze on his horse's face.

As Ramon drew nearer, the four men walked down the steps of

the verandah and out to meet him. He reined in his horse and stepped off as he told them excitedly, "Rustlers! They took nearly a hundred head of cattle." He paused for breath and then continued, "Manuel thought that he recognized Jesse Evans among the rustlers."

"How many were there?" Sam asked.

"Six, Manuel thought."

"Which way did they take them?"

"He thought they were probably headed for the Gap," Ramon told him. "They've gotten close to twenty-four hours start on us."

"Let's saddle up." Sam and the others headed for the corrals and Ramon led his horse behind them. He would saddle a fresh mount and be ready to ride with the others.

The women in the house heard the commotion and ran to the verandah to see what was happening. "What's up, Sam?" Carolyn shouted.

"Jesse Evans has taken about a hundred of our cows and we're going after them. Manuel thinks they headed for the Gap and the Bonito Valley."

While the men saddled their horses, the women quickly gathered provisions and canteens for them to take with them. It could be a long while before they returned.

Within a few minutes, the five men were loping their horses away from the headquarters toward the Gap. When they reached the steeper slopes which led to the pass through La Sierra, Lone Wolf commented grimly, "Manuel was right, the tracks are headed for the mountain; I'd have thought they'd head north."

The men slowed their horses to a steady walk as they began to climb. The mountain trail and the forest grew thicker as they climbed.

"Keep your eyes open for an ambush," Thor cautioned as he watched the tracks.

However, the summit of the Gap was reached without incident, and they started down the south slope as they followed the clearly visible tracks made by the cattle. Occasionally they saw the shod tracks of the horses which the rustlers rode.

When they reached the foot of the Gap, the tracks turned east along the base of the mountain. "They're following the Base Road," Ramon said, "which way to you think they'll go from there?"

"It's anybody's guess, so far," Sam commented. "They could go down the southside of the mountain or drive them on to the

134

Bonito Valley. We'll soon know."

They followed the tracks to Salazar Canon and then followed them to Double Crossing where they turned eastward, keeping to the north side of the Bonito River. Now they could see where the rustlers had held the herd for the night, on a meadow close to the river. The tracks were clearly visible in the softer ground of the valley and they followed them until they reached Lincoln Canon. Sam and the others had half expected to find the tracks heading farther south through Priest Canon, but they still continued eastward.

"I half expected them to go over the hills to San Patricio, thereby missing the people down the valley," said Sam.

The men now entered the Lincoln area and rode around the cultivated fields which lay on the north side of the town and river. Jesse Evans, if it were indeed he, had felt no such compunction for the hardworking farmers, and the tracks of the cattle were easily followed through the trampled crops.

Alvino Gonzalez was inspecting the damage which the cattle had done to his alfalfa and vegetable crop when the group rode up.

"The gringo outlaws went down the valley," he yelled in frustration. "I hope they did not do as much damage to my neighbor's fields."

"How long ago did they pass by?"

"So early that the bawling of the cows woke us up and it was just daylight," Alvino told him, "don't bring them back, Senor Sam; plant them under some rocks somewhere when you meet up with them."

"Report what damage they have done to your crops to the sheriff, Alvino; it will be an added charge against them," Sam suggested.

"Huh?" Alvino looked at Sam in surprise, "Why don't you tell me to report the damages to Senor Evans himself? It's the same thing, no?"

Lone Wolf glanced at Thor and they both chuckled. "He's got a point there," Thor said as he turned in his saddle to look at Sam.

"I guess you're right," Sam replied disgustedly, as he touched his horse with his spurs.

"There's Billy the Kid tying his horse to the hitching rack by the Tunstall Store," Ramon said as he pointed across the river.

"Yeah, and that looks like Dolan walking up the street and keeping his eye on the kid as he walks," grinned Thor.

"There's going to be a big blowup soon," Ramon predicted. He continued to look toward the little town which sat on higher

135

ground above the river. "I hope Senor Chisum and Tunstall will be the winners."

"They can fight all they want over the government beef contracts and political power for the area as long as they leave us alone," Sam said.

"Eventually we will have to take sides," Thor told him.

"Maybe," Sam replied, "but until that time comes, we'll stay out of it."

"There's Juan Patron near the torreon." Ramon waved at the store owner who was waving at the S-F men and pointing down the valley.

"He probably thought that the cattle were being driven legally," Ramon said.

"Until now, he might have thought they were being driven legally, but it's obvious he doesn't think that now."

"Shall we cross the river and report the rustling of our cattle to the sheriff just to have it on record?" Ralph looked inquiringly at his father.

"He knows about it," Ramon said. "He probably saw them go by and waved his blessing at them."

"It will be legal this way," Sam decided.

"You're right there; it's always best to have the law on your side," contributed Thor.

"Having the law on your side is fine, but whose side are the law officials on?" wondered Lone Wolf.

The men forded the shallow Bonito and rode up the small slope just east of the torreon and down the main street of Lincoln toward the office of the sheriff and the jail. When they reached the sheriff's office, they dismounted, tied their horses at the rack and entered the building. "Where's the sheriff?" Sam asked of the deputy.

"He's gone to Fort Stanton to see Colonel Dudley." The deputy rose from beind the desk as he spoke.

"Tell him when he returns," Sam said grimly, "that we're on the trail of Jesse Evans and the cattle that he stole from us."

Sam walked over to the underground cell and glanced down into it. "Keep that pit ready. I hope to bring you some boarders," he told the young deputy.

The cell was a rock-lined pit dug in the ground. Its ceiling was level with the floor and the only access to it was through a trap door.

"I'll do that, Sam," the deputy told him.

As the men left the jail house, Alexander McSween rode by. "Having trouble, Sam?" he inquired.

"Nothing we can't handle," Sam told him.

The S-F riders mounted their horses and trotted them down the dusty road until they reached the Ellis house.

"Let's cross the river again and stay with the trail," Sam suggested. Once more they splashed across the mild little Bonito and followed it eastward. The tracks were easily discernible as they passed through cultivated fields lying beside the river.

"We're not the only irate hombres around here," commented Thor grimly as he surveyed the damage done to the crops. Damage done almost maliciously.

The trail led doggedly eastward, past the junction of the Bonito and Ruidoso rivers. Now the enlarged river was called the Hondo, and they still rode eastward until the tracks finally turned off at Alamo Canon, heading in a southwesterly direction toward Apache country.

"Apparently they plan to sell the cattle to the reservation, or maybe they plan to go on through to Tularosa and sell them there."

Sam leaned forward and folding his hands on his saddle horn, continued, "One thing is for sure, they won't go any farther east, for that's Chisum's territory and no one would buy stolen cattle down there."

"They may be taking them to El Paso or on to Mexico," Ramon suggested. "It isn't that far from Tularosa to the Rio Grande."

"Could be," Sam conceded, "no one would ask questions about the brand in Mexico, but that's a long way to trail only a hundred head, unless they're planning to add to the herd as they go."

"We'd better catch them before they hit big timber," Thor said.

In answer, Sam spurred his horse lightly and loped up the canon in front of them. Now the sign was fresh and the rustlers couldn't be far ahead of them.

"There's a small cupshaped meadow not far into the canon," Ramon told the others. "It could be there that the cattle are being held."

After they had ridden at a mile eating trot for several minutes, they could pick up the faint sounds of cattle bawling in the distance.

"We'll swing around behind those hills and come up on them from the top of that knoll." Sam reined his horse to the right and began to climb the gradual slope of the small hill. The vegetation was sparse in this area and when the men neared the top of the hill, they left their horses ground tied and went on foot for the remainder of way. The smell and sounds of cattle were plain now as they slowly edged upward and peered over the knoll. They studied the situation in silence and then they quietly slid back under cover of the hill to confer.

"I got three. What about the rest of you?" Sam looked around the circle.

The others nodded in agreement, for only three riders were visible as they watched the cattle. Sam now motioned for them to move back toward the horses, and went on, "It is my guess that they are holding them here until some more cattle arrive; what does it look like to you?"

Ramon spoke first in a low voice, "They are part of the Evans gang, all right, and it is my guess that Jesse and a couple of his men left to get some more."

"That's my reasoning, too, and we'd better act before the others return," Sam decided.

The other four agreed and Sam continued, "Let's circle them and close in when I do."

They left quietly and each circled the small hills surrounding the basin until they were in the positions designated by Sam. He waited until he judged they were ready and then began to ride down the hill, all the while keeping his eyes fixed on the three outlaws.

The outlaws, apparently feeling quite safe from pursuit, had built a small fire and were gathered around it. As Sam rode down the steep hill, his horse's hoof loosened a small rock which rolled down the rocky hillside, alerting the rustlers. They leaped to their feet, their hands on their holsters as they looked up at Sam. Now four shots rang out from four different directions, and the outlaws realized Sam wasn't alone. Sam continued to ride toward them with his cocked rifle pointed at them. Now Ralph, Ramon, Lone Wolf and Thor rode in tightening the circle. They, too, had their rifles ready.

When he had reached speaking distance, Sam spoke in a flat, unemotional voice. "Fools die at an early age."

The rustlers thought it prudent to raise their hands.

"Get their guns, Thor," Sam said as he watched Thor step off his horse and approach the three.

"Where's Jesse?" Sam asked.

"Who?"

"Tie them up, boys," Sam ordered, "and lay them at the entrance of this little valley, and then stand clear because I'm going to stampede the cattle right over them."

"That's cold-blooded murder," one of the outlaws howled as he was being tied.

Thor and the others hustled the outlaws toward the entrance to the small basin-like valley where they would tie their legs together. "Give us five minutes and then we'll join you and make sure the cattle go in the right direction," called Ramon.

"Wait! Jesse left about two hours ago and headed down the Hondo. Some of the boys are bringing some cattle up from the Pecos to add to these."

"Whose cattle are they bringing up?" Sam asked.

"Chisum beef," came the reply.

"How many?" barked Sam.

"How many? I don't know . . . as many as they could gather, I guess," another volunteered.

"Leave them there under those juniper trees," Sam called, "until we get back."

Within a few minutes, the S-F men were retracing their steps toward the Hondo where they swung eastward along the south side of the river. They reached Picacho without spotting any sign of driven cattle and rode on down the river. Before they reached Sunset, they could hear the sound of bellowing cattle and the faint sounds of gunfire. They put their horses into a lope and before long saw a good sized herd stampeding up their side of the valley toward them. No one had to tell the experienced frontiersmen to take to higher ground as the cattle passed, and they waited, expecting to see riders following them. No one appeared and now once more they heard the sound of gunfire from the direction of Sunset which was a small settlement a short distance to the east. The men spurred their horses down the slope and galloped toward Sunset. As they turned the last bend in the valley before reaching Sunset, the shooting suddenly ceased. The S-F men reined in their mounts and listened and could hear hoofbeats rapidly approaching, and then they saw horsemen racing up the barren side of a hill just in front of them.

"That looks like Jesse in the lead," Ramon shouted, "Chisum's boys must have given battle."

"Identify yourselves," a voice suddenly called to them.

"Don't shoot . . . we're from the S-F . . . Jesse rustled some of our cattle, too," Sam answered.

"Come on in," the hidden voice yelled back.

"Merry Christmas to you, too," Sam answered. "You identify yourself first."

"Is that you, Sam?"

"Could be . . ." Sam replied, "and who might you be?"

John Chisum rode his horse out of the thick stand of trees which lined that section of the Hondo river.

"So it is you, John." Sam and the others rode into the open also.

The men from the two outfits had a short palaver and then they all rode up the valley to gather their respective herds.

The Chisum cattle were spread out over a considerable area of the valley where it widened and the Chisum men began to push them together as the S-F men continued on up the valley toward Alamo Canon.

"I think we'll leave the cattle there for tonight," Sam decided. "They've been chased around enough for now."

When they reached the cattle, they found the three rustlers were gone. They speculated as to how they might have gotten loose and decided either someone had happened by and taken pity on the outlaws who might possibly have friends in the valley, or some other member of their gang had freed them. Whatever had happened, it seemed to be out of their hands to exact justice. The S-F men hoped that the rustlers might think twice before running off any more of their cattle.

Long before sunup the following morning, the men began the slow drive back to the ranch. They decided to take them back around the eastern end of the mountain, thus avoiding where possible, the little settlements and their cultivated crops. This they did and the drive home was without incident.

CHAPTER XIX

"**R**iders coming in from the east, Sam," Ramon called out, "six, maybe seven of them."

Sam reined in his horse and waited for the approaching men to reach them.

"Hello, Sam," a familiar voice yelled when they had reached hearing distance.

"John Chisum! What brings you this way?"

"Cattle, as usual. I'm afraid we've both lost a large bunch," John told him as he and his riders pulled up their horses.

"Rustlers?" Sam questioned in anger.

"No," replied Chisum, "this time buffalo carried them off."

"What do you mean? I've never known the herds to come this far west in recent years. I know they used to graze this country all the time many years ago, but since the white man has settled here, they have stayed clear."

"For some reason one of the herds wandered onto our cattle range and took hundreds of my cattle and I'm sure some of yours, also, with them when they turned east. I have no stomach at my age to go looking for them. It would be impossible to cut the cattle out of the buffalo herd once we located them anyhow," said Chisum.

"When did the herd take them? Have you any idea?" asked Sam.

"As near as I can figure it, they must have come in a week or so ago. They might have stampeded . . . I don't know about that. All I know is we saw plenty of evidence of their passage through the eastern part of your range down through mine. I just thought you and your neighbors would like to know about it," Chisum continued. "You're not thinking of going after them, are you Sam? Because if you are, you're foolish. Messing with those hairy beasts can be dangerous and deadly."

Sam sat his horse and was silent, obviously thinking.

"Count me out, Sam," Chisum said, "but if you do decide to go after your cattle and are lucky enough to rescue any of them, you are welcome to any of mine that you're able to cut out. Well, I'll be heading back to the ranch. Good luck, Sam, you'll need it."

Chisum leaned over to shake Sam's hand and he and his men turned and rode away the way they'd come.

"If you're thinking of going after the cattle, Sam," Ramon said as they watched the receding riders, "I know of an old buffalo hunter who might advise us."

"Is he close by?"

"He lives on the Hondo River since he gave up the buffalo. His name is Sofio Herrera."

"Let's go back to the headquarters and get Lone Wolf and Thor and head for the Hondo and ask Sofio some questions and get his opinion, what do you say, Ramon?"

"John Chisum is getting too old and set in his ways, too cautious. He didn't build his empire by being that cautious. I say at least talk to Sofio."

When the S-F men reached the junction of the Hondo River, they turned east for a mile.

"That's Sofio's place over there, up against the south side of the hills." Ramon pointed to an adobe house which had chickens scratching for food around it. A dog which was sleeping beside the front door raised his head and pricked his ears and began to bark furiously as the men approached. A milk cow grazing in the meadow adjoining the river raised her head and looked at the approaching strangers. The front door of the house opened and a tall, grey haired man stepped out. He carried a rifle under one arm.

"Hello, mi amigo," Ramon called. "Como esta usted?"

"Ramon!" Sofio responded. He leaned his rifle against the side of the house and walked out to greet his friend, extending his hand for a handshake. "Muy bien, gracias, Y usted? Get down and come in. To what do I owe the pleasure of your visit? Welcome to my casa, such as it is."

"He lives alone," Ramon told the others, before he turned back to Sofio. "We have come to speak with you about the buffalo."

"Let's sit under the tree and talk; it's much cooler there," Sofio replied as he led the way toward a giant old cottonwood.

Ramon now introduced Sam, Thor, and Lone Wolf to his friend as they sat down in the welcome shade.

"A buffalo herd came onto my grazing land north of the mountains and carried off some of my cattle. Do you think that it is feasible to try to get them back?" Sam asked.

"How many cattle did they take?" Sofio asked.

"Don't know for sure, but John Chisum seems to think it could be in the hundreds," Sam replied.

"That's a sizable number," Sofio returned, "you may never see them again, senor, but it is possible that we can get some of them back, if conditions are right."

"What would those conditions have to be?"

"Buffalo are dangerous and unpredictable animals. They move into the wind because their eyesight is poor, especially when their eyes are also covered with wool and surrounded by flies and gnats. They depend on their noses for safety you know, that is why they always move into the wind. Sometimes the flies and gnats form huge clouds over the herd just after the breeding season or during the winter; we could catch them broken up into small bunches, and it would be easier to move in and cut the cattle out. If the cows were dropping their calves, it would be a good time to move in also, because the bulls separate themselves from the cows at that time. If your cattle are with the cows, it will be hard to cut them out because of the mother instinct to protect their young. It would have been easier to cut them out of the bull herd then if they are all together as they will be. This time of year, they'll all be together, but considering the number of cattle that you believe they took off, I'd say it would be worth at least a try at getting them back," Sofio concluded as he looked at his guests.

"How many men would we need?" Sam inquired.

"We have more than enough men right here. Buffalo can smell humans long before they can see them, so the fewer humans we have the better. That will be to our advantage. Many times I have gone buffalo hunting by myself. In Comanche country one person will not be detected as easily as a larger number of people. My neighbor, Porfidio Silva goes out on the Llanos with me, but more often than not, we both prefer to hunt alone."

"Let's give it a shot," Thor said. "Sam, if we find the buffalo herd that stole our cattle and Sofio checks it out and thinks we can cut out some of the cattle without too much trouble, I say we do it."

Sam next looked at Lone Wolf who replied with a laugh, "That's one thing I've never done in my life, been to a rodeo where I had to cut cattle from a herd of buffalo. I'm game!"

"And you, Ramon?" Sam asked.

"Hey, since when have I backed away from a challenge? My ancestors have done the impossible many times, and I am part Spanish, am I not?"

"Good," Sam said with satisfaction. "When do we start, Sofio?"

"In the morning," Sofio replied with a grin. "I'll get my Big Fifty out and check it over."

"I've always wanted to see one up close," said Sam. "I know it is a special rifle which Sharpes made for buffalo hunting, but that's about all."

"A slug from the Big Fifty has been known to travel up to five miles," replied Sofio. He grinned, "The Indians call it the gun which shoots today and kills tomorrow."

Early the next morning, way before dawn, the five men rode east down the Hondo Valley and finally up out of the valley and onto the rolling foothills heading for the Pecos river valley.

"I'm sure the herd will be east of the river," Sofio told them as they rode along. "Are any of you familiar with the Llano?"

"A little," Ramon replied, "but very little. I went out there once with my father and some others from the Torrez Ranch when I was a small boy."

"And the rest of you?" Sofio inquired.

The others shrugged and Sofio continued, "I see; well then, I will give you a quick lesson as we ride along. If we get separated and you become lost, remember we are riding east and we have come from the west. If it is a cloudy day, so cloudy that the sun cannot be seen, remember that the wind almost always blows in from the southwest. See, how the grass leans away from that direction? Look also at the other vegetation . . . most of it leans also. Tonight, I will show you which two stars of the Big Dipper point to the North Star. If the stars cannot be seen, feel for the wind or breeze. Remember, though, that sometimes it can play tricks on you and change direction.

"When the sun comes up, the calm, cool air combines with

the little moisture which has collected during the night and can cause you to see things which aren't there, so beware of mirages.

"I'm sure you all know of the northers which can drop the temperature fifty to sixty degrees in a matter of minutes? A norther can also bring a blizzard or a sandstorm as you know."

They camped that night still west of the Pecos River and continued on their way early the following morning. The sun was almost directly overhead when Lone Wolf spoke, "I can smell water."

"It's the Pecos River you smell," Sofio told him as he pointed toward the horizon.

"That row of trees must line its banks," commented Thor.

"Right," Sofio replied, "but along some parts of the Pecos, you'll find no trees at all."

As the men approached the river, thousands of wild turkeys took flight, with a sound that was almost deafening to the ears.

"I guess we won't camp along the banks of the Pecos tonight!" laughed Sam.

"Not unless we want to risk turkey droppings falling on us," agreed Thor.

Before they camped for the night, they were well beyond the vicinity of the Pecos, but managed to bag a young hen turkey for their supper that night, and everyone sat around the small fire enjoying the tender bird. Finally Lone Wolf rose and said, "I'll take the first watch."

"I can tell that Indian won't let us be caught napping," Sofio said with a chuckle.

"My friends are all seasoned mountain men and Indian fighters. That's one thing you won't have to warn them about," Ramon told his friend.

"That is very comforting," Sofio replied, "people like me are not looked upon very kindly by the Indians."

They turned in shortly after that and when Thor's turn came to keep watch, he was forced to walk from one to another of the sleeping men and give them a poke, warning them in a low voice, "I can smell buffalo," he whispered to each of them as he woke them.

They rolled from their blankets and saddled the horses and packed the two mules.

"They're upwind of us," Lone Wolf said.

"They have to be because they would have stampeded if they were not," Sofio whispered.

Shortly they could hear the growls of wolves and the yapping of many coyotes in the still morning air.

"The strongest scent comes from the south, with less of an odor north and east of us," Lone Wolf whispered.

"Let's wait it out," Sam finally decided. "We'll wait until sunup and then we can see how large the herd is and if it contains any of the cattle."

Accordingly, the men waited by their horses and remained silent until the eastern skies began to lighten little by little and a cool breeze sprang up. Now they could see the outine of the herd begin to take form as the sky grew lighter.

"It's a small herd," Sam whispered, "maybe five hundred head?" He glanced inquiringly at Sofio.

"It's a splinter bunch off the main herd," Sofio returned. "I don't see any sign of cattle, do you?"

Each of them finally shook his head as their eyes searched the herd of massive, shaggy creatures as they ate their way down the broad valley.

Sofio finally motioned for the others to follow him up the valley away from the herd. Quietly and slowly the riders put more distance between themselves and the buffalo. When they were perhaps three or four miles apart, Sam asked Sofio, "How far could the rest of the herd be from those?"

"No telling, we'll just have to keep moving until we see it or signs of it," Sofio told him.

Four hours passed without seeing another buffalo; by now the men had reached the area of the cap rock. Suddenly, Ramon turned and pointed ahead of them, saying, "Buffalo?"

There was movement out there, but it was difficult to determine whether it was buffalo or not. They continued to ride in that direction for a long while and then Sofio said, "It's a large bunch of antelope . . . you can often find large herds of deer and even some elk out this way."

Now they spotted buzzards circling in the air ahead of them, some of them flapping their wings occasionally, but most of them gliding effortlessly through the clear blue sky.

The riders put their horses into a lope now and within a short time picked up the odor of rotten, decaying meat.

"I've come close enough," said Sofio as he reined in his mount. They sat their horses and watched as in the distance they could see wolves tearing at downed buffalo and magpies jumping from one carcass to another and the entire area seemed alive with

146

buzzards who had arrived to join in the feast.

"Buffalo hunters," Sofio commented, "they took the hides and left the rest. I wonder if they took the tongues."

"I for one am not going to find out," Ramon commented wryly.

"This does not concern us, anyway," Sam said. "I don't see any cattle among the carcasses."

"Buffalo robes and hides bring about two dollars and a half now, they say," Sofio mused as they rode on. "And then some of the hunters sort out the largest bulls and kill them for the trophy."

"Is there much of a market for trophies?" Ramon asked.

"Not too often. Sometimes the hunters may have been quoted a price which some easterner is willing to pay for the right head. And some people want a buffalo rug with the head attached, but most of the hunters cut the head loose from the hide," Sofio told them.

"One of these days, cow hides will be in more demand after the buffalo are thinned out," Sam said. "And that is when the rancher will begin to thrive."

"Cattle hides and beef are coming into their own now, Sam," Sofio told him, "but cattle hides will never replace buffalo hides for quality, in my opinion. Buffalo hides are softer than cow hides which makes them easier to work with. The factories back east that use leather belts to keep their machinery turning, prefer buffalo hide belts over the cow hide. So do the people who upholster their furniture with leather. But your days are almost here, Sam. The time of the rancher has arrived and the time of the buffalo is about over."

"How much farther do you want to go, Sam, before we give up the search?" Sofio asked after they had ridden many more miles.

"Let's give it another day and if we don't find any sign of the cattle by then, we'll decide then what to do," Sam replied.

"Since the coming of the settlers, the herds have changed," Sofio commented as they continued to head east.

"How have they changed?" Thor asked.

"They are much wilder now than they were twenty years ago. They spook much easier also, and once they have stampeded, nothing stops them until they have run their course. They carry everything in their path with them. The Indians now have to send scouts out continuously watching for the herds, because a stampeding herd could wipe out a village."

"What are those trail-like lines running around the sides of those hills up ahead?" Ramon questioned Sofio.

"Buffalo trails."

"There must be thirty of those rings around the hills," Ramon said, "none of them very far apart, the way it looks from here, anyway."

"When one trail gets worn down too deep, the herd leader begins another trail just above the first. Buffalos are creatures of habit, just as all other animals, including humans," Sofio laughed.

"Those trails all seem to lead down between those hills. I'll bet they lead to water, and where there's water, we might find buffalo and maybe some of our cattle," Sam said. "Let's have a look."

They put their horses to a trot as they rounded the foot of the hill. Within a few minutes they saw the first of the cattle, a small herd grazing on a meadow not far from a waterhole fed by springs. The buffalo had trampled all of the vegetation around the waterhole for at least two hundred yards.

"We're in luck!" Thor said as he rode up closer to the cattle. "Some of them branded with the S-F and some with Chisum's brand."

"There are no more than fifty in this bunch," Lone Wolf commented, "Chisum said that together we lost a lot more than this."

"The rest have to be with the buffalo herd," Sam replied. "The tracks by the water hole are not more than a day old, so the herd can't be far off."

Lone Wolf rode his horse up out of the small basin and the others watched him as he reached the higher ground. Within a few minutes, he rode back down again, "I can smell buffalo from up there."

"We've found our buffalo herd, I'll be bound," said Thor. "Now how are we going to cut our cattle out of the buffalo?"

They all looked at Sofio.

"Do you have any ideas about how to do that, Sofio?" Sam asked.

"Which do you think are faster, buffalo or cattle?" Sofio countered. "I know that buffalo can move almost as fast as a horse, but cattle cannot. Am I correct? You people are the cowmen."

"Sofio, you're thinking of stampeding the buffalo and when they raise their tails and skidaddle, they'll outrun the cattle, leaving them behind?" Sam asked.

"Why wouldn't it work?" Sofio asked in return.

"I don't see why it wouldn't," said Thor.

"Won't some of the cows get stomped on by the rushing buffalo?" wondered Lone Wolf.

Everyone turned back to Sofio.

"Some of them could get knocked down," he conceded, "but I don't think that we will lose too many that way. I think the buffalo will just run around them." He looked at Sam, "They are your cattle and it's your decision to make."

"Let's start that stampede. We'll come back to gather these later!" Sam spurred his horse up the slope and the others followed, riding in the direction where they expected to find the buffalo.

Suddenly Sofio reined in his horse and yelled "Buffalo stampede!"

The others rode a short distance farther and then came back to where Sofio sat his horse, looking puzzled. "What made them stampede and in which direction are they headed?' He went on nervously, "If they are headed in our direction, we'd better get out of their way. How easy that will be will depend upon how many are in this herd. If they number in the thousands and are spread out for miles, we could be trampled."

"There!" Lone Wolf yelled as he pointed northeastward.

"That's good,' Sofio yelled back. "Thank God they're headed east." Sofio crossed himself and continued, "It's a large herd, maybe ten to twenty thousand."

By now dust was climbing into the sky and minute by minute the dust cloud grew darker.

The others could hardly hear Sofio because the noise made by the thundering hooves had become a roar. They sat their horses and watched as the buffalo herd swept eastward.

"We'll wait until the dust settles where the stampede began and then we'll ride in," Sofio yelled. "The dust is too heavy now; we won't be able to do much under these conditions."

So they waited and when the air finally began to clear, they rode out to investigate. They trotted over one knoll after another until they reached the point where they thought the stampede had begun. They then turned their horses and followed the wake of the herd which had disappeared from sight and sound. They had traveled perhaps two miles when they sighted the first cow, and as they continued to ride toward the east, they found that more and more cattle had been left behind. They continued to follow the trail of the fleeing buffalo until finally no more cows were found to have dropped out of the vast herd.

"How many do you think we've found, Thor?" Sam finally asked.

"I'd say eight hundred to a thousand," Thor replied.

They began to gather the last of the stragglers and started them back along the way they had come, adding a few now and then as they came across them. They handled them easy, taking their time, letting them quiet down after their run, though most of them were tired and willing to be herded with no trouble.

Sam sent Lone Wolf and Ramon to gather the first cattle they'd seen and bring them back to meet them, as they eased the main bunch in the direction they planned to take on the way home.

"A lot of them carry Chisum's brand," Thor observed, "maybe seventy percent of the brands I've read are his."

"Not many others but his and ours, but we'll see that our other neighbors get theirs back," Sam told him.

"What caused the stampede? That's what I'm wondering," called Sofio. "Could have been Indians?"

"No sign of Indians as far as I've seen," replied Sam.

"Well, something caused them to hightail it," Sofio said as he rode over to Sam's side of the herd. "We'd better try to find out why, before we expose ourselves on the plain. There's no sign of a prairie fire, no thunder storm or tornado, and no sign of Indians, and they could not have picked up our scent because we were too far away. Did anyone hear gunfire?"

"I didn't," said Sam.

"It couldn't have been buffalo hunters, then, and the only other reason they might stampede is flies and gnats. Sometimes they get so bad, covering the faces of the buffalo, that they can't see. They get down into their hair and bite their hides and crawl up into their noses and ears. The buffalo are finally maddened by it and the only way they can shake them is by stampeding. That must have been the reason this time."

Late in the afternoon, after they had joined up with Ramon and Lone Wolf and the rest of the cattle, Sam suggested that they make camp. "If we get a good start in the morning, we should be able to move them fifteen miles or so tomorrow. They've had enough for one day."

A small fire of buffalo chips was started to heat the coffee and jerky was passed around as that evening's meal.

Slowly, they made their way back toward the ranch. As they approached the Pecos River, Sofio said, "You can see the Sierra Blanca mountains in the distance with old Baldy still covered with snow. Pretty as a picture, isn't it? It must be close to a hundred miles from here and over there are the Capitan Mountains. 'The

Mountains that Stand Alone' the Indians call them, although most people call them the Capitans now. We Hispanic people still prefer to call it La Sierra, though."

As they neared the Pecos, Thor and Lone Wolf searched for the best place to ford the river and when it was found, the herd was taken across the river.

"We're nearly home," Thor said with satisfaction as the last cow reached dry land on the west bank of the Pecos. "Probably sixty miles to go, but that's not far." He looked toward the distant Capitans and commented, "I'd never heard that the Indians called it the 'Mountain that Stands Alone'." He looked over at Sam, "How did it get that name?"

"It is said that the Indians called it that because even though it's not far to other mountains in the area, it still stands aloof from the others, the Sierra Blancas and the Jicarillas. It won't be called that for long, though, for the Indians are probably on their way out," Sam said soberly. "That could be our loss."

He went on in a happier vein, "I'm itching to get home. You'll come with us, won't you, Sofio? You might grow to like the place and us, and you're welcome to stay on permanently. Everyone needs a family, and you live alone and we would consider it our gain if you would become a member of our family."

"Man was not meant to be alone," Ramon added, as he looked at his friend. "Join up with us. These are good people; you cannot find any better."

Sofio nodded in agreement.

EPILOGUE

By the late 1800's, Lincoln County had become the scene of the Lincoln County War. The names of Pat Garrett, John Tunstall, William Brady, John Chisum, Alexander McSween, Billy the Kid and James J. Dolan were better known to the outside world than the hard-working ranchers.

Murder, violence, theft of cattle and property on a grand scale had become part of life. Many settlers left, fearful of what the future might bring but others, like the Sidwells, stayed. They had an unshakeable faith in the eventual triumph of good. This was their homeland, the place of their roots. They were determined to pass that heritage down to their children and their descendants.

In time, Indians and outlaws as well as the mountain men became part of western legend and myth. But the land remained and the families, like the one founded by Sam and Carolyn, flourished. In the long run it is their story that is the true story of western history.